3 4028 08229 1379
HARRIS COUNTY PUBLIC LIBRARY

YA Cassid X
Cassidy, Anne
Killing Rachel

WITHDRAWN

$16.99
ocn794367528
03/20/2013

KILLING RACHEL

Also by Anne Cassidy

The Murder Notebooks: Dead Time

The MURdeR NoTeBooKS

KILLING
RACHEL

ANNE CASSIDY

WALKER BOOKS
AN IMPRINT OF BLOOMSBURY
NEW YORK   LONDON   NEW DELHI   SYDNEY

Copyright © 2013 by Anne Cassidy
All rights reserved. No part of this book may be reproduced or transmitted
in any form or by any means, electronic or mechanical, including
photocopying, recording, or by any information storage and retrieval
system, without permission in writing from the publisher.

Published in Great Britain in March 2013 by Bloomsbury Publishing Plc
Published in the United States of America in February 2013
by Walker Books for Young Readers, an imprint of Bloomsbury Publishing, Inc.
www.bloomsbury.com

For information about permission to reproduce selections from this book, write to
Permissions, Walker BFYR, 175 Fifth Avenue, New York, New York 10010

Library of Congress Cataloging-in-Publication Data
Cassidy, Anne.
Killing Rachel / Anne Cassidy.
    pages   cm. — (The murder notebooks ; [2])
Summary: As her stepbrother, Joshua, continues to decipher the meaning of the
cryptic murder notebooks, Rose wonders if the recent death of her former best
friend may hold a clue to the disappearance of Rose's mother and Joshua's father.
ISBN 978-0-8027-3416-7
[1. Missing persons—Fiction. 2. Murder—Fiction. 3. Ciphers—Fiction.
4. Stepfamilies—Fiction. 5. London (England)—Fiction.
6. England—Fiction. 7. Mystery and detective stories.] I. Title.
PZ7.C26857Ki 2013   [Fic]—dc23   2012027189

Typeset by Hewer Text UK Ltd., Edinburgh
Printed in the U.S.A. by Thomson-Shore, Dexter, Michigan
2 4 6 8 10 9 7 5 3 1

All papers used by Bloomsbury Publishing, Inc., are natural, recyclable
products made from wood grown in well-managed forests. The manufacturing
processes conform to the environmental regulations of the country of origin.

To Alice Morey and Josie Morey
My favourite teenagers

ONE

Rose was hiding. It was dark and cold and she was in a shop doorway staring at two people across the road. The street was busy and a stream of people passed without noticing her, wrapped up against the cold night air. She could see clouds of white breath coming from their mouths and hear their excited chatter as they talked about their plans for the evening.

She kept her eyes on the couple.

The boy was her stepbrother, Joshua. He was standing outside a door next to a cafe called Lettuce and Stuff. Opposite him was a girl who Rose had never seen before. She was shorter than Joshua and was wearing a kind of duffel coat with the hood down. Her fair hair was spilling over her shoulders, and she was staring up at him, seemingly rapt. The sight of it gave Rose a sore spot in her throat.

It was just gone seven and she'd been on her way to Joshua's flat. She had arranged to eat with Joshua and Skeggsie, his flatmate. She'd been looking forward to it and rushed so that she would be on time. She was early, in fact, but she knew it wouldn't matter. Joshua and Skeggsie wouldn't mind what time she got there. She'd just sit at the kitchen table while they cooked and talked. When Joshua had invited her round he had said they should keep off one particular subject. They were going to try very hard and not talk about The Notebooks. The notebooks had been all consuming but now it was time for their lives to get back to normal after what had been a dramatic few weeks.

Walking along Camden High Street she'd been pleased to see Joshua on the pavement outside his flat. It was almost as though he'd had some second sense that she was on her way. She was ready to smile and quicken her pace but a stranger had stepped out of Joshua's front door.

A girl.

Rose stopped in her tracks and watched as seconds later the girl was joined by Joshua. Rose crossed the road on to the other side and walked along until she saw the recess of a shop doorway. She stepped into it and watched them talk.

Five minutes went by and they were still talking.

She became angry with herself for not walking straight up to Joshua and saying, *Hi, Josh* and *Hello* to this girl and then going upstairs to see Skeggsie. Now she would feel embarrassed. She glanced upwards to the first floor of the building. She half expected to see Skeggsie's face at one of the windows staring down at her. There was nothing, though; just the warm yellow light of the kitchen. She should be up there now.

She thrust her hands into her pockets crossly. In one she felt the corner of an envelope pressing against her skin. It was a letter that she'd been carrying round with her all day. Her grandmother, Anna, had handed it to her as she left for college. When she realised that it was a letter from her old boarding school, Mary Linton School for Girls, she'd felt instantly apprehensive. She'd shoved it into her coat pocket intending to open it later when she had time, when she felt up to it. She'd left it in her pocket all day long. She'd not quite *forgotten* about it. It had buzzed around the edges of her thoughts all day, an annoying but persistent presence. It was only when she set off for Joshua's that it went out of her mind.

Now it sat in her pocket unopened, silent, bearing a message of some sort that she didn't particularly want to hear. She recognised the handwriting so she knew exactly who had sent it.

She let her fingers run over it and felt the linen paper that Mary Linton used for its stationery. It reminded her suddenly of the school's administrative offices, the place where you went if you had a query about your parents' visits or if you were being picked up for a trip out of the school grounds. The tables in the waiting area had thick blotters on them and small wooden letter stands with headed notepaper and envelopes. The paper was light blue and felt luxurious. The envelopes were thin and long and opened at the top of one end. They had to be stuck down by licking the gum. The stationery was like the boarding school: old-fashioned and expensive.

Rose realised that the girl talking to Joshua was standing closer to him. There was no gap at all between them. She looked like she was going to *kiss* him. It would only take a second for her to go on tiptoes and angle her face up to his. Or he would just lower his head and place his lips on hers. Rose held her breath. The traffic had stopped and although people were walking past they were a blur to her, so fixed was she on the two people across the road.

She felt her heart twist. Were they going to kiss?

They did not. Seconds later the girl backed away and walked off and Rose felt a swooning sense of relief. Her eyes followed the girl as she wove in and out through other pedestrians and finally disappeared. Across the road the door to Joshua and Skeggsie's flat was closing. She moved her shoulders about, loosening her clenched muscles.

Rose, Rose, she thought, *what's the matter with you!*

Joshua opened the door and smiled at her.

'Right on time,' he said.

She walked in and felt the heat of the flat. In front of her was a steep staircase and she followed Joshua up until she came to a tiny landing. The smell of food was in the air.

Skeggsie appeared. He had a bibbed apron on over his shirt, tie and trousers. His black-rimmed glasses made him look like a scientist but he was an art student, though nothing like any artist that she had ever pictured. His face was red and in one hand he had an asthma inhaler and in the other a spatula. He didn't say hello, or call her by her name, he simply said, 'Food's ready.'

As Rose and Joshua walked past him he sucked on the inhaler.

'Don't mix those up, Skeggs,' Joshua said.

Skeggsie managed a smile. Rose caught Joshua's eye. Skeggsie enjoying a joke was not something she'd seen often.

They ate hungrily. No one mentioned the notebooks. It was the first time in weeks that it hadn't been the main topic of conversation between them. The narrow kitchen was hot and Rose took her jumper off, draping it over the back of her chair. The butterfly tattoo on her forearm stood out and she focused on it for a moment. It had completely healed now and looked as though it had always been there. A Blue Morpho butterfly. A reminder of her mother, who she hadn't seen for five years.

Skeggsie was talking about the animation course he was doing at college and how he had plans to make a short film. Joshua was nodding and picking at his chicken with his fingers. He had his sleeves rolled up and his shirt was unbuttoned showing a grey T-shirt. She stared at his chest. There, underneath the T-shirt, on the left side of his ribs was *his* butterfly tattoo. The first time he'd shown it to her she'd traced her fingers along it, feeling the outline of the image. She wondered if he sat in front of a mirror and looked at the delicate picture imprinted on his skin; larger and more dramatic than hers. She pictured him staring at it and thinking of his father, Brendan, who he hadn't seen for five years.

Skeggsie's voice interrupted her thoughts.

'So, this guy in college is going to collaborate with me on the film!' he said.

Rose and Joshua immediately looked at each other. Skeggsie had a *friend*. Someone in college that he liked and trusted enough to work with. Joshua read the surprise on Rose's face and did a mild shrug as if to say, *First I've heard of it*, as Skeggsie continued talking about Pixar and classic Disney and French animation techniques.

Later they ate pieces of cheesecake and it seemed as though the conversation had run out. This was the time when they might have slipped back into the ins and outs of the notebooks as they had done for weeks. Instead they sat silently and Rose ate her cheesecake, one spoonful after another.

'Who was that girl I saw, earlier, walking away from the front door?'

She *hated* herself for asking.

'That was Clara, from school.'

Is she your girlfriend?

'Is she on your course?'

Joshua nodded.

'Clara is an odd name,' Rose said lightly. 'What's it short for?'

'Dunno,' Joshua said, sitting back, placing both hands on his stomach, as if he was full up.

When the meal was over she helped Skeggsie wash the dishes and put them away in their allotted places. Then she decided to go back to her grandmother's house.

'Great meal, Skeggsie,' she said, getting her coat and bag.

'I'll walk you to the station,' Joshua said.

'No need.'

'I don't mind.'

'I'm a big girl. I can walk the streets of London by myself!'

She spoke a little more sharply than she had meant to and Joshua put his hands in the air defensively.

'Sorry,' she said, walking down the stairs.

The front door was not bolted. She was getting used to this. Skeggsie, who had previously been paranoid about having the door locked every time someone came in, had relaxed somewhat.

'Skeggsie still all right with the door?' she said, her voice a bit lower in case he heard.

Joshua nodded. 'Plus he's got this new mate at college. Looks like he's finally coming out of his shell.'

'Um . . .'

It had taken Rose a while to take to Skeggsie and she still wasn't quite sure about him. But he was Joshua's friend and she had to accept him as he was.

'Going anywhere this weekend?' Joshua said.

'Got a lot of work to catch up on. You?'

'There's a thing at college I might go to.'

Was he going out with Clara?

'I'll email you. Maybe I'll drop by on Sunday or something.'

She paused for a moment. 'We managed not to talk about the notebooks.'

He nodded. 'Doesn't mean we weren't thinking about them.'

'No,' she said.

He grabbed her hand and squeezed it. She smiled and then stepped out into the street and gave him a backward wave. Walking along she let her fingers curl up, for a second imagining what it would have been like to grasp his hand back. She shook her head at her own stupidity and headed for the station.

She opened the door to her grandmother's house and went into the hallway. She called out, not expecting an answer. Anna had been out a lot in the last couple of weeks and it meant that Rose had the house to herself. She walked straight upstairs to her rooms and shrugged her coat off on to a chair. Then she remembered the letter from Mary Linton School for Girls that she had yet to open.

She reached into her coat pocket and pulled it out.

It was from Rachel Bliss.

Dear Rose,

You will be surprised to get this letter from me but I have no one else to turn to. We had our bad times in the past but I am a different person now and I want you to know that I am sorry for any hurt I caused you. I am writing because something horrible is happening to me. It's hard to explain. I don't understand it myself. You're the only person I can turn to, the only person I can trust.

This is not a cry for attention, I promise. I have this terrible feeling that something bad will happen.

Please ring me on my mobile.

You did like me once. Please don't let me down.

Rachel

Rose read it over three times.

She frowned and screwed the letter into a tight ball.

TWO

Rose spent Saturday morning on her laptop. She was trying to catch up on her work. Weeks before, she'd had time off from college and missed some assignment dates. It was important to her to get back on track. She had English assignments to finish and some prep for Art. Plus there was reading and making notes for History and Law. It had all slipped behind and, instead of being one of the top students, she was being nagged for overdue work.

When she heard the front door she went out on to the landing. Her grandmother was standing in the hallway looking flushed and pleased with herself. She smiled up at Rose.

'Do you want a coffee?' she called up.

'OK,' Rose said.

Rose went into her room and closed down the document she was working on. She had a quick look at her emails but there was nothing new. Then she went downstairs and into the kitchen. She didn't really want a coffee. She'd accepted the offer because in the last couple of weeks a change had come over her grandmother and it involved her making coffee for Rose three or four times a week. It had started oddly one evening when Rose was working in the small room attached to her bedroom which she used for a study. Anna had tapped on the door and entered with a small tray on which sat a white mug and a small cellophane packet of biscuits. The mug had a high shine, its handle angular. It was part of a set that Anna had on display in the kitchen. She had drunk the frothy coffee and dunked the biscuits and wondered why her grandmother was being so much more sociable. In the days that followed Anna had called her down to the kitchen a number of times and made her a drink and sat with her. There had been conversation and it became clear to Rose that Anna was *making an effort* with her.

'Black OK?' her grandmother said.

Rose nodded.

It had been different in the past. They had had some bad arguments where Anna had said upsetting things about her mother and Brendan, Joshua's father. There had been days when Rose had wanted to walk out of the door of Anna's house and never come back.

Now it seemed as though Anna was getting to know Rose for the first time even though she had, in fact, been under her care for five years. When Rose's mother and

Joshua's father disappeared Rose met her grandmother for the first time and came to live with her. There followed years at Mary Linton School for Girls, where she was a boarder and spent short periods of time with her grandmother. They were not close but now it seemed her grandmother was trying to be different. So even though Rose didn't always feel like a coffee she made herself sit down and drink it.

'I may go away for a few days,' her grandmother said, after some small talk about Rose's courses.

'Oh?'

'There's a couple of concerts I'd like to go to at Snape Maltings. I thought I might go on Friday morning and have a long weekend with a friend of mine.'

'OK,' Rose said, nodding encouragingly.

Her grandmother took a few moments to tear the cellophane on the small packet of dark chocolate biscuits. Rose looked at her grandmother's nails, perfectly manicured and polished, each nail having a half circle of glitter at the tip. Her nails were always like this. Her clothes were conservative, bought from Bond Street, but her nails could have been done in Camden Market and they rivalled those of many of the loud, brash girls at her college.

'I used to go for weekends a lot when you were at Mary Linton but since you've come back I haven't been.'

'You should go,' Rose said.

There was quiet for a second and her grandmother's

lips twisted to one side as if she was hesitating about what she was going to say.

'I wonder,' she said slowly, choosing each word with care, 'when I'm away, if you wouldn't mind, I'd prefer it if that boy, that *Joshua Johnson*, didn't come into this house.'

Rose stiffened.

'He's my stepbrother . . .'

'Not your *stepbrother* as such . . .'

'We lived together as a family . . .'

'But your mother did not marry his father so you are not related to him. Not by law or by blood.'

'I think of him as my family . . .'

'I know that. And I know that you see him and he visits you in your studio and I have to accept that but I really do not want him here in my home. It just doesn't feel right to me . . .'

Rose pushed her mug away.

'Don't get upset, Rose,' her grandmother said. 'You said a few weeks ago we should be honest about things and I'm just trying to tell you how I feel.'

'My getting upset is me being honest,' Rose said.

'So, we're both saying what we feel. Maybe that's a good thing? Both being honest? Wasn't that what you wanted?'

Later in her room Rose thought about what Anna had said. Her grandmother's attitude to Joshua had been upsetting Rose for weeks. Anna had always been antagonistic towards him. Rose knew Anna had strong feelings about Joshua's father and these had coloured her view of this boy who she had never met. Rose wished Anna could see how great Joshua was. How caring and thoughtful he was. How driven he was to find out what had happened to her mum and Brendan. Rose wished that Anna could see Joshua the way she did.

But these thoughts did not make her feel better.

Lately Rose's own feelings towards Joshua had developed into something that made her feel deeply uncomfortable. When she'd first heard from him six months before she had been overwhelmed with joy at the thought of having one part of her family back in her life. When she met him again for the first time in five years it had seemed so natural, so meant to be. He had been missing from her life and then he was back and together they had been a team. Stepbrother and stepsister on a search for their parents.

But Anna was right. He wasn't her stepbrother.

He was Joshua and her feelings for him had become mixed up. Her emotions had taken on a kind of longing for him that she couldn't control. It had started weeks before when they had been through some difficult emotional times. They'd been there for each other and Rose had come to lean on Joshua. But one day she had felt those feelings edge into dangerous ground. There was even a moment when she had been drawn towards kissing him. Just in time though she'd pulled back, retreated to a safe place.

They were family.

She had no right to have any other kind of emotional attachment to Joshua. Standing close to him in the queue for coffee or the cinema she could feel the heat coming from him, smell the scent of spearmint gum and hair shampoo and sometimes she wanted nothing more than to bury her face in his skin. It was those times that she found herself thinking more and more about the fact that they were not really *related*.

But it was unthinkable and she had to push those feelings down.

That's why it was better to keep busy, to get her school work up to date. She opened a document on her laptop and looked through the notes she'd made earlier. After a few moments she heard footsteps on the stairs and a light knock at the door.

'Post,' her grandmother said.

Rose exhaled slowly. It was another letter from Rachel Bliss.

'I didn't think young people corresponded in this way any more,' her grandmother said, handing it to her.

Rose waited until the door closed behind Anna before opening the letter.

Dear Rose,

I realised, after posting my letter yesterday, that you might think I had gone mad. Maybe I have.

Strange things are happening to me, unexplainable things.

I've been thinking a lot about Juliet Baker. I can't seem to get her out of my thoughts. I need to talk to someone about it and you are the only person I feel I can trust.

Please write to me and send me your mobile number – then I can call. I'm begging you.

Rachel

Juliet Baker. That was a name that hadn't come into her mind for a long time. She lowered the letter and sat very still, thinking back to the last time she'd seen Rachel Bliss.

In Mary Linton School for Girls the bell rang for the change of lessons. Rose heard it in a detached way. Now that she was leaving it no longer resonated with her. The sound of footsteps could be heard from the corridor below her room. Lines of girls moving quietly from classroom to classroom. After a few moments the noise of movement subsided and she continued packing her belongings into large trunks. She'd already filled two and was now on to the third. Many of the things she was packing would be dumped as soon as she returned to her grandmother's house: her uniform, lots of the stupid girly clothes that she'd bought, soft toys that she'd accumulated, books and magazines and piles of cards and letters and photographs that she had amassed over the years of being a Mary Linton Girl.

She heard the door open behind her. She turned and saw Martha Harewood, her housemistress, standing there.

'Nearly done, Rose?'

'Almost.'

Martha walked across the room and sat on the edge of Rose's bed.

'I'll be so sorry to see you go. I know you were upset a few months ago but I thought that had been sorted out . . .'

'I'm all right, really. I just want to get back to my grand-mother's. I guess I'm just tired of boarding.'

'At least you've taken your exams.'

Rose nodded. She'd taken all twelve of them in the previous weeks. Now they were over and there was nothing to keep her at the school.

'I still think this has something to do with Rachel Bliss.'

Rose shook her head.

'We used to be friends but we haven't been close for a while. It has nothing to do with my leaving.'

Martha stood up.

'Well, it's good to see you so grown-up, so well. Not like the sad young girl who arrived here.'

Rose took some moments smoothing down the corner of a folded blouse. *Sad young girl.* Martha was referring to the months after she first came to Mary Linton. The days when the ache for her missing mother was like a sickness. Martha had been there then, always with a box of tissues handy and a hot chocolate which she made just for the two of them in her rooms. Martha had been ready with a gentle hug and soothing words. Martha had just been *there*.

'You will come and see me before you leave?'

Rose nodded.

The door closed behind Martha and Rose was alone. She finished packing, then stripped her bed and folded up the laundry and piled it in the corner of the room. It was 12.15 and her taxi was due at one. On the side of her trunks were giant labels: *Rose Smith, c/o Anna Christie, 17 Andover Avenue, Belsize Park, London.* She was going to live full-time with her grandmother. In the autumn she would become a student at the local high school and she and Anna would see each other every day. She wondered how that would be, how they would rub together.

Her door opened suddenly and Rachel Bliss stood there. She didn't speak but looked around Rose's room, her eyes resting on each trunk. Rose stared at her. Rachel's hair was loose, flicking up on her shoulders. It looked white and made her face paler than usual. Her blue eyes took in the whole room as if she'd never seen it before. She was wearing cut-off jeans and flip-flops, weekend wear. Around her neck was a heart-shaped locket on a chain. Rose stiffened. She had bought it for Rachel the previous year.

'Really going?' Rachel said.

'Yes.'

Rachel gave a little smile. She was still at the door as if she didn't want to come into Rose's room, as if there was an invisible barrier keeping her out. She lifted her arms, her hands at the back of her neck.

'I wanted to return this,' she said.

She unfastened the locket and chain and held it out in her hand.

Rose didn't move. 'I don't want it.'

'Neither do I,' Rachel said and tossed it in her direction.

Rose watched it fall on the carpet as Rachel walked away, her flip-flops making slapping sounds on the floor along the corridor. Then she picked it up and held it tightly in her palm. Her eyes felt sore but she would not cry. Not any more. She went across to the bin and threw the piece of jewellery into it.

Now, five months later, it felt as though Rachel Bliss was standing at the doorway of her study in Belsize Park, staring at her with steely blue eyes. She read over the last line.

I'm begging you.

Rachel.

She folded the letter over and over. Then she folded it again.

THREE

Rose and Joshua were in the studio at the bottom of Anna's garden. It had once been a garage of sorts. It was brick-built and run-down but when Rose left boarding school for good she had restored it and made it a place of her own. She kept her art equipment there and it was also big enough for an old sofa, a wicker chair and several big cushions. It was Sunday evening, just after seven. Joshua was lying across the sofa, his big boots hanging off the end. Rose was sitting on the floor, resting her back against the battered upholstery. On the floor were two plates and the remains of takeaway noodles. There was a rolled-up magazine by the plates, and a can of beer and a bottle of Coke. Music was playing in the background, one of her favourite bands. After eating and drinking she had told Joshua about the letters she had received from Rachel Bliss.

'This is the girl who upset you in Norfolk?'

She nodded.

'And she wants you to help her?'

Rose didn't say anything. It wasn't really a question. She'd told Joshua some stuff about Rachel in emails she'd sent months before.

'Well, I'm not replying . . .' she started saying.

'Oh! I got this letter,' he said, interrupting, sitting up and struggling to pull a folded envelope out of his back pocket, 'My Uncle Stu forwarded it. From the solicitors? Myers and Goodwood?'

The solicitors who acted on behalf of their parents.

'See what it says.'

He passed the letter to her. She read over a short paragraph.

Dear Joshua,

I'm sending this to your uncle as I don't have your current London address. I hope you are well and that you are enjoying your university course.

Some items of your father's property have been sent to us. If you ring me (you have my mobile number) and give me your London address, I'll forward them to you.

Yours

Robert Myers

'Oh,' she said.

'I rang him yesterday,' he said. 'They have something of

Dad's from seven years ago when he was working in the area headquarters at Chelmsford. Do you remember? He went there for three months? He had to stay over some nights?'

Rose shook her head. She honestly didn't remember. Both her mother and Joshua's father had been in the police force. Rose had known that but she'd had no idea *where* they'd worked.

'He was based there for three months. Now they're reorganising and the offices are to be used for something else. They needed to clear stuff out and found a file of Dad's. They sent it to the solicitors.'

'There's nothing from my mum?'

Joshua shook his head, 'No, it was just Dad who went to Chelmsford. Kathy was still working in central London.'

'I don't remember.'

'You were only ten.'

That was true. At ten she hadn't thought much about her mother's job. She knew her mother was a police-woman but she didn't go out and walk the streets like the police officers who came into her school. She often felt a little cheated by this. Her mother went to work in a dark suit with high heels. She looked like any businesswoman going out to work.

'I wonder what it is?'

'Who knows? I gave them my new address and they're

going to send it to me. Maybe it's something that will help us find them.'

Finding their parents.

It had become the main thing for both of them. It had always been Joshua's passion but Rose had spent five years packing away her emotions and trying to get on with her life. She had been so sure that her mum and Brendan were both dead, murdered because of some cold case investigation that they were working on.

She had been told this by a senior policeman weeks after they went missing. She remembered that visit as if it was yesterday.

Chief Inspector Munroe had come after she'd been living at her grandmother's house for a few weeks. He was an important and busy man but this visit was something personal, something he had to do.

'I worked with your mother and Brendan. That's why I had to come and see you face to face,' he said.

He was in uniform and sat opposite her in the drawing room. He placed his hat on the coffee table between them. His face was tanned as if he'd just returned from a holiday. He pulled at his collar a couple of times, giving her an encouraging smile. He looked uncomfortable. No doubt he wished he was back on the beach. Her grandmother was moving quietly around behind her and she could hear the clink of cups and saucers on a tray. Rose waited for Inspector Munroe to give her some information, some news about her missing mother. Her grandmother placed two cups and saucers on the table. On each of them sat a silver spoon.

'I'll be in the other room if you need me.'

Her grandmother spoke quietly and Rose wasn't sure if she was addressing her or the policeman.

'How old are you, Rose?' he said, moments later, his voice soft.

'I'm twelve.'

'You're going to have to be a very grown-up girl because I have some very bad news to give you.'

Rose stared into his eyes. Her throat felt hot as if it was on fire. The policeman went on in a low and unhappy voice.

'There were four ongoing investigations in the Cold Case Ops Team. We have looked into the ones where your mother and Brendan Johnson were the leading officers and we have come to the conclusion that they touched a nerve somewhere. It's our view, after reviewing all the evidence, that they are most certainly dead, killed by an assassin, paid for by organised crime.'

He stopped and looked at her as if he expected her to say something.

'Have you found their bodies?' Rose said, imagining her mother's face still and pale, her eyelids tightly closed.

'No. I doubt we will ever find them.'

'Then how can you be *sure . . .?*'

'All the evidence points in that direction. Things we have found out which we are not yet able to make public. If we did it might harm other investigations. Your mother was an excellent police officer, Rose. I knew her. I knew her years ago when she first started working for the force. She was very professional. She would have understood this. You are a young girl but you must understand it now.'

Rose lowered her face and sipped at the burning hot tea. She kept her eyes on the tanned man opposite her. He fiddled with his cup and moved around in his seat. Chief Inspector Munroe. She'd never heard her mother mention him before.

'What's your first name?' Rose said.

He looked taken aback.

'My name is James. James Munroe,' he said, pulling something out of his pocket. 'Here's my card. Feel free to call me at any time. And I would add that I will continue this investigation for as long as it takes to determine what happened to your mother and Brendan Johnson.'

She took the card and looked at it as Chief Inspector Munroe stood up. Her grandmother had reappeared as if by magic and their voices faded in her ears as she focused hard on the words in front of her. *Chief Inspector James Munroe*. She wondered if Joshua was sitting in his uncle's house in Newcastle with another nice policeman sitting nearby saying, *I will continue this investigation for as long as it takes to determine what happened to your father and Katherine Smith . . .*

Now Rose knew that it wasn't true. The policeman had been wrong. The past back then had been a place of darkness, a black hole which had sucked their parents down. Now there was some light. They had found out that her mother and Brendan were *alive*. They hadn't *seen* them nor did they know where they were but they'd been told that they were safe and Rose and Joshua were determined that they would find them. She felt emotional all of a sudden and turned to say something to Joshua about it but he had his eyes closed.

Later, when it was time for Joshua to go, she tidied up the plates and picked up the can and bottle. Her knees were stiff and she stretched her arms out. It felt like it was late at night. Joshua was saying something to her.

'You're not thinking about that girl from school, are you?'

'Rachel? No.'

'She really upset you, didn't she?'

Rose nodded.

'Lucky you've got better friends now, then!'

'Friends? I thought we were family?'

'We are, but we're friends as well,' he said, throwing an arm around her shoulder and giving her a swift hug.

He went out of the gate at the bottom of the garden and Rose waved at his disappearing back. It was quarter to eight. She wondered if he was going back to the flat or if he was heading off somewhere else. The blonde girl, Clara, came into her head. She was a friend from uni, he'd said. Was Joshua heading off to see her? The thought of it made her throat dry.

The music was still playing in the studio and she slumped down for a moment on the sofa where Joshua had sat. On the floor she saw the envelope that his letter had come in. She picked it up. His name and his uncle's address were on the front. At the bottom right-hand of the envelope, in italics, was the name of the solicitors, *Myers and Goodwood*.

It wasn't exactly an unforgettable name and yet it was one that Rose had heard often over the years. *Myers and Goodwood*. They had a will that her mother and Joshua's father had made. This had been explained to Rose in the early days of living with her grandmother. Two years or so before they disappeared her mother and Brendan had made a contingency will. It stated that should anything happen to them then the financial affairs and well-being of their children would be dealt with by the solicitors. It wasn't unusual, a solicitor had told Rose, for officers involved in dangerous work to make provisions for their families in case anything unexpected happened.

And something had happened. They had vanished into thin air.

There'd been a babysitter that night, a girl from along the street, Sandy Nicholls. Rose was allowed to stay up and wait for her mother's return and she'd sat next to Sandy on the sofa, linking Sandy's arm as they watched programme after programme. From time to time Sandy pressed the *Mute* button and told Rose some gossip from school and some story about a boy she loved who was treating her badly. Sandy also spent a good bit of the evening tapping out texts on her phone. Eventually, as the evening got later and later, Sandy rang Rose's mother's mobile but it just went to voicemail. Rose remembered her leaving a message. *Hi, Mrs Smith! It's just me, Sandy. Nothing wrong here. I just wondered when you were planning to get back. Only it's 11.15 now and it's a little later than you usually stay out!*

Joshua came down from his room where he'd been for most of the evening. He avoided making eye contact with Sandy and gruffly asked, 'Where are they?'

Rose watched Sandy walk back and forth to the window, pulling the curtain to the side and looking out. Joshua sat in a chair in the corner staring at his mobile and looking up now and then, his face turning towards the door expectantly.

After midnight Sandy rang her parents. At one o'clock Sandy's father came round. Mr Nicholls had a wobbly stomach and a loud voice and he sent Sandy home and told Rose and Joshua to go to bed. He said he'd wait up for their parents.

There was nothing else to do but go to bed. Rose got under her duvet and called out to Joshua. He came to her room.

'Do you think they're all right?'

'Yeah.'

'You don't think they've been in an accident?'

'Nope. The car's broken down most probably.'

'Why haven't they rung?'

'Probably both their phones have run out of charge. They know we'll be all right. You go to sleep. When you wake up they'll be here.'

She went to sleep almost immediately. When she woke it was early morning, still dark. The clock on her bedside table showed the time as 6.27. From downstairs she could hear murmuring. A low conversation was taking place in the room below her. She got up and went to the door of her room. She opened it and saw Joshua sitting on the top step dressed in the same things that he'd been wearing the previous night.

'Are they back?' she said.

He didn't look round at her. He just shook his head.

Rose found herself gripping the edge of the old sofa, her eyes misting. Not now, she thought, she would not cry now when they'd been given new hope. She stood up and took a couple of deep breaths. She put the rubbish in a plastic bag, turned off the heater and the music, and went out of her studio and closed the door firmly behind her. She walked round a laurel hedge and up towards the house. The light was on in Anna's drawing room. She had friends round. Rose had nodded politely at them as they arrived.

She went into the kitchen and washed the plates. The drawing room door must have opened because the sound of people talking and laughing got louder. Anna came into the kitchen.

'There's a message for you on the answerphone. From one of your friends at Mary Linton. Sounds like a nice sort of girl although a little wound up about something. It was a surprise, I must say. You don't usually get calls here.'

Rose frowned. A phone call from Mary Linton.

She dried up both plates as a feeling of anxiety took hold of her. Rachel knew her home number from the time when they'd been friends. When she replaced the plates in the cupboard she went across to the handset and pressed the message button. She recognised the voice immediately.

Rose, I'm hoping you got my letters. I'm hoping to hear from you soon. You won't let me down, will you? I'm depending on you.

Rose stood very still for a moment.

How many times was this girl going to try and contact her? She jabbed her finger on the *Erase* button and went up to her room.

FOUR

Rose didn't have a class until late morning so she decided to work at home for a couple of hours. Her grandmother had left early and the house was quiet.

The sound of the post arriving came from downstairs. She went out on to the landing and looked down to the hallway. There was a stack of letters on the hall mat. The sight of them gave her a tickle of apprehension. Underneath, at the edge, she could see a blue corner sticking out. She went downstairs and picked up the mail. She could feel the heavy linen paper underneath the pile of letters and when she placed them on the hall table she pulled out the slim blue envelope. Irritated, she went back upstairs and opened the bottom drawer of her desk. The other two letters were in there. For some reason she'd smoothed them out and kept them. She tossed the unopened envelope of the third letter in and closed the drawer.

She decided to go on to her blog, Morpho. In the last

weeks she'd not posted much on it but since recent events had given her and Joshua some new hope about their parents she'd made a decision to use her blog to document what was happening. The blog was *invite only* and at the moment she was the only person who had access to it. She thought that maybe, one day, she would share it with Joshua.

At the top of the post she typed the words **The Notebooks**. Then she sat back and pulled up her left sleeve to look at her butterfly tattoo. She'd had it done weeks before, lying to the man in the tattoo parlour about her age. It had hurt; tiny stinging movements as he drew on to her skin. *Are you sure you're all right?* he'd said a couple of times, looking concerned. The blood had oozed out in pinprick bubbles. She'd nodded for him to go on, watching each movement with fascination. She'd been overjoyed to find that Joshua had a similar tattoo on his chest, but when she discovered that Brendan had one as well as her mother it seemed unreal. It had been a strange link between them. They had all drawn blood to have this image on their bodies, like some kind of secret ritual.

She thought for a moment before starting to write. The blog was a way of her explaining what was happening, maybe even explaining it to herself. She began to recall the events after it became clear that their parents had gone.

When our parents went missing I lost touch with Josh. Even though we'd lived together as a family for three years, he was sent to live with his uncle in Newcastle and I lived with my grandmother in London. Then one day, six months ago, I had an email from him. It was the most amazing moment. We swapped emails over months and eventually we met up in London. We spent our first weeks together trying to find information about Mum and Brendan and one day we found a man who told us the most astonishing thing.

Our parents were alive.

Rose pictured this man, Frank Richards, the last time she saw him.

He was tall and thin. He travelled light with just a suitcase on wheels and a holdall. He was also a policeman and had been friends with Joshua's dad, but he'd been sacked. Neither Rose nor Joshua knew why. This was just one of the many things they didn't know about Frank Richards. They didn't even know if *Richards* was his real name. Coming face to face with him had been completely unexpected. More amazing was the fact that he also had a butterfly tattooed on his arm. When they questioned him (desperately, intensely) he'd held things back, he'd refused to answer saying *I've already said too much.*

And he had. He'd told them the one thing they'd wanted

to know. Kathy and Brendan were alive. In a single sentence he had resurrected her mother and Joshua's father and changed their lives for ever.

Frank Richards had been keen to get away from them. They'd followed him out of his flat into the street where he was trying to get a taxi to take him to the airport. He gave Rose a telephone number to ring in case of emergencies, in case she was ever in danger. *Why would I be in danger?* she'd wanted to ask but he'd jumped into a passing taxi, dragging his suitcase on wheels behind him and left. She'd keyed the number into her mobile even though she wasn't sure why she would ever want to get in touch with Frank Richards again.

Joshua had been elated by this meeting.

And thrilled with the notebooks.

We stole something from Frank Richards. In his flat he had a pile of notebooks next to his case. There were about six, like exercise books. Inside were photographs and maps and diagrams. There was a lot of writing but it was all in code. There was also a battered copy of an old hardback book called The Butterfly Project. While Frank was packing his stuff, Josh hid two of the notebooks in his coat. We can't understand the code but we're trying. Our friend, Skeggsie, tried to crack it but he came to the conclusion that the code was linked to an 'unknown'

source. Maybe a book that was held by all partici-
pants of the code. We immediately thought of The
Butterfly Project.

A couple of weeks after they'd met Frank Richards she
had gone round to the flat and found Joshua and Skeggsie
in a state of excitement. On the kitchen table, laid out
in front of them, were the two notebooks. She looked at
the notebooks for the hundredth time, letting her
fingers play around the edges. One notebook was closed
but the other was open showing a photocopy of a photograph. The face was that of a man of about fifty. He was
thin and he had cropped grey hair and he was looking at
the camera rather than posing for it. His eyes were dark
and his eyebrows heavy. He had on a white shirt and
dark tie and a suit jacket as if he was on his way to some
formal event.

They'd had no idea who this man was. Skeggsie had
used his computer to access facial recognition systems
but his hardware did not have the scope to link up with
bigger sites and he'd found nothing.

'Tell her, Skeggs,' Joshua said excitedly.

'This guy at college? He has access to the college hardware. He works part-time there, blah, blah . . .'

Rose wrinkled her eyebrows. Skeggsie had begun to use
the words *blah, blah* whenever he couldn't be bothered to
explain something.

'So I asked him if he could put this photo through the college computers.'

'And?'

'He found a match.'

'Wow. Who is he?' she said, staring at the face of the man in the notebook.

'His name is Viktor Baranski. He's Russian,' Joshua said and carried on. 'We've googled him. He was a former Russian navy man. He came to London in 2000 as a businessman. He bought property in Mayfair and Kensington and mixed with people in high places. Skeggsie looked at some Russian newspaper archives at the time he came to Britain and there was some suggestion that he sold information to the British government. Information about the Russian navy.'

'Skeggsie can read Russian?' she said, impressed.

'Got it translated,' Skeggsie said dismissively.

'The thing is,' Joshua went on, 'he was murdered in 2006. He was found washed up on the Norfolk coast. Skeggsie read that he might have been killed by the Russian secret service as some kind of payback for giving information to the west.'

Rose blew air out through her teeth. It was too complicated.

'What's this got to do with Mum and Brendan?'

'Well, they may be involved with the secret service? MI5?'

'James Bond? It's a bit far-fetched.'

'Just about everything to do with this stuff is far-fetched,' Joshua said, his voice falling. 'Why should this be any more unreal?'

'Anyway,' she said, trying to be positive, 'it's great that you found out who the guy is. It's a start.'

'Not me. Skeggsie.'

Skeggsie looked up at Rose. Rose gave a grudging smile.

'Thank you very much, Mr Darren Skeggs, blah, blah,' she said, using his full name for the first time.

'You're welcome, Miss Rose Smith, aka pain in the backside.'

'That's what I like to see,' said Joshua. 'You two guys getting to like each other.'

Joshua now thinks that our parents may have been working for the government. It sounds weird to say it but he believes that they may be spies or spooks, whatever they're called now (not 007).

She stopped typing because the house phone was ringing.

She sat back in her chair. She should answer it but she didn't want to in case it was Rachel Bliss again. Anyone who wanted to get in touch with her would use her mobile or her email. It might just be for Anna and whoever it was would leave a message. She waited until the phone stopped ringing and looked back over what she'd written on the blog.

> I don't believe our parents are spies. I think it's a ridiculous thing to say but I can't explain that to Josh because he is so driven, so passionate about finding the truth. It's really because of him that we've found so much out. It was because of him that we found Frank Richards, mostly. It was because of him that we got hold of the notebooks.

The phone rang again.

Rose tensed. She just *knew* that it was Rachel Bliss. She looked round and wondered what to do. If she answered it maybe she could tell her to leave her alone and that would be that. On the other hand Rachel – if it was Rachel – might pull her into something, might say something that Rose wouldn't be able to ignore. Better if she left it to ring and then she could just erase the messages as soon as she heard Rachel's voice.

She looked back to the blog, reading over the last couple of paragraphs, distracted now, not really remembering where she was in this story.

> Joshua thinks that the notebooks are everything.
> They are the key to finding out more. I'm not so

sure. There a number of reasons why I think the notebooks are not so important.

1. Who uses notebooks for important things? When there are laptops and memory sticks, email and so on.
2. Frank Richards was an odd man. Maybe the notebooks are specifically to do with him. Maybe they don't link to Mum and Brendan at all.
3. Who uses code? In this day and age?

Maybe the notebooks are red herrings and we are wasting time trying to figure out what they mean.

Reading over what she'd written made her feel guilty – as if she was mocking the things that Joshua said, the theories he had. She should be less negative. If it hadn't been for him they would still think that their parents were dead, killed because of some cold case they were working on. She ended her blog.

We are certain we will find out more about the notebooks.

The phrase *The Notebooks* had become, to Joshua, shorthand for *finding out about their parents*.

The sound of the phone ringing again startled her. It seemed louder this time as if the person ringing was determined to be heard. Rose made little fists with her hands and then stood up and walked stiffly downstairs. She picked up the receiver and put it to her ear. The ringing stopped. The silence was soft and enveloping and she didn't speak, just listened. Rachel Bliss's voice was scratchy as if she'd been crying.

'Rose? Is it you, Rose? Oh, Rose, you have to speak to me. I feel like I'm going mad . . .'

Rose replaced the receiver.

She went upstairs feeling gloomy. She had no idea how she was going to stop this girl from harassing her. No idea at all.

FIVE

On Tuesday morning Rose opened her wardrobe door and looked at her clothes. A line of black trousers, jeans and skirts hung from the rail. Alongside them were white shirts and tops with several sweatshirts, cardigans and jumpers folded below. After she left Mary Linton School for Girls she had started to dress in this plain way. She liked the clarity of the monochrome, the sharpness and cleanness of the way they looked together. Anna hated it and tried to persuade her to buy colours. Even Joshua commented on it from time to time but she was adamant. She dressed how she wanted to dress and no one had the right to tell her what she should wear.

Every now and again though she saw something in a shop, a soft pink or turquoise and she felt drawn towards it, imagined wearing it, pictured it against her skin. Once she'd even taken a pink silk blouse as far as the till but had changed her mind and placed it back on the rail and left the shop feeling silly.

Now she fingered the trousers and jeans and wondered what to wear. She pulled out a pair of trousers and a white T-shirt and baggy cardigan. She picked her boots up from the floor and opened her drawer and took out a pair of bright purple socks. These could be worn but not seen.

Maybe one day she would wear colours openly.

Before leaving for college Rose opened the drawer of her desk and took out the unopened letter from Rachel Bliss. The phone calls had unsettled her. It was bad enough hearing messages that had been left but worse to pick up the phone and hear Rachel speaking to her. Not speaking to her, *appealing* to her.

The letter sat in her hand. It would be just like the other two. Rambling words trying to pull her in, to make her care, to get her to do Rachel's bidding.

She opened it wearily.

Dear Rose,
Things are bad for me, very bad.
Over the last couple of weeks I've seen Juliet Baker four times.
I really have.

Rose paused. This was just another of Rachel's lies. She sighed loudly and carried on reading.

I already told you that she's been on my mind a lot lately.
Anyhow, it was late at night and I was looking out of my
room towards the lake, staring into the dark and suddenly
she was there under the trees, just beyond the car park. I
was so shocked. Her face seemed to shine in the dark.
She was standing there. I kept my eyes on her, afraid to
look away, and she was still, like a statue. Her face was
white against her hair, like there was no blood in her at
all. She seemed to stare me out and in the end I had to
look away and when I turned back she was gone.
It scared the life out of me. I couldn't sleep.
Then yesterday I was in the quad trying to read a book
and I looked up at my room window. Juliet was there.
Her face was there staring down at me. She was at my
window, Rose! She was in my room. I was hysterical.
I ran up there. I just charged through everyone else
and ran like mad. When I got there the door was shut.
I opened it and the room was empty.
So now you will think I've gone mad.
You see why I need your help.
Please contact me, Rose.
Rachel

Rose lowered the paper, her face crinkled. *Juliet Baker.*
How on earth could Rachel have seen her? Juliet Baker
was dead. She'd been dead long before Rose ever set eyes
on Rachel Bliss. What was Rachel saying?

That she had seen a ghost?

Ridiculous.

Rose pulled her laptop out of her bag and opened it, logging on quickly. She went on Google and put in the words *Juliet Baker Mary Linton School for Girls*. After a few seconds a number of entries came up. She clicked on the *North Norfolk Gazette*.

Day Boarder Commits Suicide

A day boarder at a private girls' boarding school was found dead by her brother yesterday. The girl, Juliet Baker, fifteen, had attended the school since she was eleven. The girl's father, Philip Baker, was a gardener at the school until recently. The head-mistress, Mrs Harriet Abbott, said that the staff and students were dreadfully upset and that this was a tragedy for the school and the family.

The girl's body was found in the garage of her parents' home.

Her parents and brother are being comforted by relatives.

Rose looked at the small photograph at the corner of the page. It showed a smiling schoolgirl. She had pale skin and black hair which hung to her shoulders. She had a fringe which threw a shadow over her eyes. Her teeth looked very white.

Rose never knew this girl. Juliet Baker had been in Brontë House and although she must have seen her around she couldn't have been in any of her classes. She knew about her, of course. When the suicide happened the whole school had crumpled. There were pictures of her everywhere. Her pale face and dark hair gave her a look of melancholy, as if somehow she knew she was going to die young. Every time Rose walked round a corner she seemed to see the girl's face staring at her. The death disturbed everyone. The teachers went around dabbing their eyes, their faces red, their voices scratchy. Many of the students went into hysterics and although Rose felt sad for what had happened she had no connection with this girl and had just kept herself to herself while the melee continued.

Eventually things got back to normal.

Then, a while later, Rachel Bliss moved out of Brontë House and joined Eliot House, and Rose and she became friends. She'd known that Rachel had been one of Juliet Baker's friends; they'd talked about her. It was a tragic story and hearing about it had given Rose the confidence to tell Rachel about her own past. Rachel had sat impassively while Rose had explained to her about her mother and Brendan's disappearance. At first she had been full of sympathy but then Rose had found her researching it on the internet, fascinated by any details she'd found. She remembered Rachel calling her into her room, her eyes glittering with excitement, to show her various news-paper reports on her laptop; **Senior Police Officers Disappear; Cold Case Police Officers Vanish; Mystery of Absent Police Pair; No Clue to Police Pair's Disappearance.** Rose had been astonished. It was the first time she had seen these old newspaper articles. She hadn't even known, at the time, that the press were reporting it. She and Joshua had lived with foster parents for the first couple of weeks after their parents' disappearance and then she had gone to her grandmother's. She'd been twelve years old, aching with loss, no interest in television or newspapers. Seeing it there, years later, she'd been amazed and appalled to see her mother's name, *Inspector Katherine Smith*, in print. Then, after looking at new stuff day after day with Rachel, she'd felt herself overwhelmed by the information.

'I don't want to look at any more of this,' she said to Rachel one day. 'It's too upsetting.'

'Sure,' Rachel had said, looking concerned. 'I won't find anything else. I didn't know it would upset you. I'll just leave it.'

'Thanks. It's in the past. I don't want to keep thinking about it.'

'I know. It was insensitive of me.'

'Hey, I know you were doing it for the right reason. I know that. But just no more, OK?'

'No problem.'

But Rachel did keep looking. Weeks later Rose went into her room when she wasn't there and saw her laptop up and a Google search for *Katherine Smith* and *Brendan Johnson*.

'Why are you still researching this?' she demanded when Rachel came back into the room.

Rachel stiffened, glancing at the screen and then back to Rose. She took a scrunchie from her pocket and pulled her hair back off her face. She shrugged as if it didn't matter, as if it was inconsequential.

'This is *my* family . . .'

'Yeah, sure. I won't look any more,' Rachel said, snapping shut the lid of the laptop.

'You do understand, don't you?' Rose said.

'Whatever,' Rachel said, walking out of the room.

Then Rachel had found other dramas to talk about so she left Rose's past alone.

Rose picked up the letter again.

Now Rachel had a new drama. She was being haunted by the ghost of her dead friend.

Later, at college, Rose made an uncomfortable phone call to her grandmother.

'Hello?'

'Hi, Anna . . .'

'Rose? Is there anything wrong?'

'No, no, I was just calling because I wondered if you would do something for me?'

The words did not come out easily. Rose was not accustomed to asking Anna for a favour.

'Of course.'

'I've got a problem.'

'A problem?'

'This girl I used to be friends with at Mary Linton? Her name was Rachel Bliss?'

'Yes . . .'

'Well, she's been writing to me and ringing me. She sounds upset. She keeps asking for my help and . . .'

'She sent you the letters?'

'Yes. Thing is I'm a bit worried about her. I feel like she might be having some kind of breakdown. I don't feel that I can actually help her from here.'

'You'd like *me* to speak to her?'

'No, no. I wondered if you would ring the school and speak to the housemistress, Martha Harewood? You could just say that I was worried that something was up with her and ask her if she'd speak to her. I don't want to do it myself . . .'

'I understand perfectly. I'll do it now.'

'Thank you.'

Rose ended the call. Her grandmother was going to sort it out. She could imagine her making the call. *Put me through to housemistress Martha Harewood. Ah, Miss Harewood, I'm ringing on behalf of my granddaughter Rose Smith* . . . She should have felt relieved

but instead felt a little ashamed. She'd shoved her problem on to someone else. What else could she do,
though? She did not want to get involved with Rachel
Bliss again.

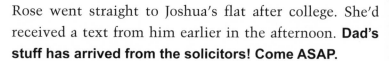

SIX

Rose went straight to Joshua's flat after college. She'd received a text from him earlier in the afternoon. **Dad's stuff has arrived from the solicitors! Come ASAP.**

Joshua opened the door.

'Come on,' he said, sounding impatient.

She followed him up the stairs, taking off her coat as she went.

It was on the kitchen table. It was a buff-coloured foolscap file. It looked old, its corners battered. A label had been stuck to the front flap but had been torn off, leaving scraps of white. On one corner was handwriting – *B. Johnson. Cold Case Ops North London.*

'I already unpacked it but I wanted you to do it as well. To get a big surprise.'

She looked a little sceptical.

'Go on, look at it!'

She put her bag on one of the chairs and picked up the file. It was heavy. She lifted the flap and she could see the edges of a hardback book. When she pulled it out she saw exactly why Joshua had been so excited. It was *The Butterfly Project*.

'Oh, wow!' she said, taken aback.

It was the same edition as they had seen in Frank Richards' flat. It was old, its pages thumbed, some turned over.

'And there's other stuff, look,' Joshua said, taking the file from her and unpacking it on to the table.

There were six things. The first, the book, sat at the far end. The others were lined up and Rose's eyes rested on each of them. There was a large photograph of Joshua and his dad, the type that might once have been in a frame. Joshua was very young, five or six, and he was sitting on Brendan's knee. It was a Christmas picture because there was a tree at the side and Brendan had a paper hat on. There was a leather key ring with a 'B' on it and a Chubb key attached. A notebook was the next thing. It was quite different to the other notebooks they had. It was half the size and had Brendan's writing in it, no code. Written in it were place names in North Norfolk. Some of them were familiar to Rose. There was a CD of Bruce Springsteen. The last thing was an Ordnance Survey map of the North Norfolk coast.

Joshua picked up the map.

'Look at the marks on this!'

He held it out for Rose to see. She expected to see Xs here and there but there were none.

'Look, tiny dots, in felt tip. See, green and red?'

Then she did see them. Dots along the coastline near a village called Stiffkey.

'What does it mean?'

'I don't know. Dad left these things behind when he finished working at Chelmsford. Someone else probably packed this stuff together thinking that Dad would pick it up but he never did.'

'Do you recognise any of the things?'

'I never saw him with the book. Nor the notebook. But the key ring I do know. I bought it for him. And the CD . . . Dad loved Bruce Springsteen. He had all his CDs. He'd been to see him in concert. He knew the words of all his songs off by heart and he used to turn it up really loud when we were driving along and sing. It was embarrassing.'

'I don't remember that!'

'No, he didn't do it in front of Kathy. She hated loud rock music and was always telling him to turn it down.'

'Oh.'

It was a strange thing but the comment unsettled Rose. She didn't like to think of her mother and Brendan at odds over anything. In her mind they had been perfect for each other. She remembered it like that. She was sure of it. She looked round to see Joshua holding the key ring by the leather fob. He was staring at it.

He was upset, she realised. These things were of some interest to her but for Joshua it was more important.

Pieces of his father's life turning up out of the blue, like sea-wrack washed up on a shore.

She picked up *The Butterfly Project*. She opened it on the first page.

'I never knew there were so many species of butterflies.'

'Um.'

Joshua was very still. He had the key ring in the palm of his hand and was looking at it oddly.

'You all right?'

Was he going to cry? He said he had bought the key ring for his dad. Was he thinking of a happy time when he gave it to him? She knew what that was like. Sorting through her drawers at home she might happen on an old scarf of her mum's and find herself instantly tearful.

'Josh, you OK?'

He sat back with the key ring sandwiched between his palms.

'Something weird is happening to me.'

She put the book down and went close to him. He was hunched and looking distracted. She reached out her hand and laid it lightly on his shoulder. She could feel the tension there.

'What's up?'

'It's too embarrassing to even talk about.'

'What? Is it to do with this?' she said, gesturing towards Joshua's father's belongings.

'If I tell you you'll laugh.'

'I won't.'

'I bought this for Dad, right?'

She looked at the key ring that he was holding in mid-air.

'A birthday present. He already had a key ring and he said he would use it for his work keys.'

Rose waited to see what else he had to say.

'I don't know if he did or not and that's not really what I'm trying to tell you . . .'

Joshua looked awkward.

'I'd better start at the beginning. Come with me. There's some thing I want to show you.'

He led her into his bedroom. The small room was tidy but the duvet was at an angle, one corner dipping down on to the carpet. Some of Joshua's clothes were laid across his hanging rail rather than on hangers. He went straight to a small chest of drawers by his bed and pulled open the bottom drawer. He sat back on the bed and pulled out a jumper. He held it up to Rose.

'This was Dad's. I packed it with me before we left the house. I've had it with me ever since. I don't wear it. It's miles too big but I have it near me, wherever I live. Years ago – and this is the bit you'll laugh at – I slept with it.'

He looked away and she felt her heart soften. She stepped across and sat on the bed beside him. She wanted to give him a hug. She raised her hands for a second but then let them drop. It pained her to see him upset but her mixed-up feelings for him made her tentative and unsure of how to act around him.

Brendan's jumper lay across Joshua's lap. She took it from him. It was huge and Rose was reminded of Brendan's size. A tall man, he seemed to stoop as he went into rooms. He had a rounded stomach and was always standing sideways in front of the mirror in the bedroom and patting it. She saw him standing on and off the scales in the bathroom several times just to check they were right. She remembered something he said regularly to her. *Diet, Monday, Petal*. He winked as he said it, which had embarrassed her at first but she'd got used to it over the three years that they'd lived together.

The jumper was maroon and had a V-neck. It was old and looked as if it had been washed too often, though not perhaps in the last five years. The wool had formed little baubles and there was a pull near the bottom.

'That's nothing to be embarrassed about,' she said.

'There's more, though.'

'What?'

Joshua didn't speak for a minute. He seemed to be debating something inside his head.

'If I tell you this you must never tell anyone. God! This is ridiculous. I'm supposed to be a *man of science*. I believe in mathematics, in logic. I think the world is made up of explainable things. I want to build bridges. Instead I'm . . .'

'What?'

'This jumper. Sometimes, when I held it close to my face, when I was lying in bed or just taking a nap . . .'

Rose looked at the jumper with puzzlement. She had no idea what Joshua was getting at.

'Well, I see this place. No, that's wrong. I didn't *see* it as such. I kind of smell it, hear it, taste it. Not every time. Just now and then. I become aware of this *place* and I am sure, I am positive it has something to do with Dad.'

'I don't understand . . .'

'I haven't done it for a long time but when I did I had these sensations. There was a smell, a taste. I heard things. I closed my eyes and I thought I could see Dad there.'

'Where?'

'I don't know. At the place.'

Rose didn't answer. She didn't get it. Then she did.

'You mean like a second sight?' she said, incredulous.

'I don't know. I've never told anyone and I wouldn't have mentioned it to you but when I picked up the key ring I had the same feeling. Just for a few seconds.'

'I don't believe in *second sight*.'

'Neither do I! I'm the last person to believe in something like that. I haven't touched this jumper for a long time because I've been trying to get it out of my head.'

'It's probably a memory that's triggered by a smell or something.'

'The key ring doesn't have a smell.'

'But you bought it for him? Right? So probably there's some unconscious link between buying the key ring, the jumper and this place, wherever it is.'

'I shouldn't have told you. You think I'm ridiculous.'

'I don't. I just think there's got to be a logical explanation.'

They were both quiet. It was the second time today that she'd been faced with some sort of supernatural phenomenon. First the ghost of Juliet Baker in Rachel Bliss's letter and now this. It was stupid. She just didn't believe in it. She must have had a dismissive expression on her face because Joshua shook his head and then turned away. It made her feel bad. He'd confided in her and she'd batted it away, made little of it.

'This place. Where is it? What is it?' she said.

He kept his back to her.

'Go on, tell me. Whether it's this *second sight* or just some deep memory of yours, it might be worth exploring.'

He shrugged but then he started to talk.

'I had this sense that it was an old cottage, or bungalow. Anyway, it was low and really old, crumbling. And it was always cold and there's masses of sky. Like the sky is everywhere, huge. And there was this smell of the sea but the sea wasn't there. It was far away. And I heard seagulls.'

'There're seagulls on Camden High Street,' Rose said.

'I know but it seems like they're *meant* to be there. Not just some scavenging birds. It's like their noise is the main thing. There's no sound of traffic or sirens or anything. Just seagulls.'

'And are you there? With your dad?'

'No, that's the point. If I was there then it would be a memory of some sort. But it's a place I've never been to. That's why it seems as though it's a signal of some sort. A sign?'

'You can't know you've never been there. I don't remember a lot of stuff from when I was young.'

'I know, I know. I just had this *feeling* that it was an important place for Dad. It's not easy to explain.'

'I don't believe in the supernatural.'

'Neither do I,' Joshua said miserably.

Rose went into the kitchen and picked up the key ring. It was solid and the letter 'B' was big and heavy. The key that hung off it was a dull brass colour. She held it for a moment and felt the cold metal. From behind she heard footsteps.

'Just forget I ever said anything.'

He walked over to the kitchen table and collected up the items from the file. She knew she'd hurt his feelings. She took a step towards him but he had his back to her. In any case, what could she say?

'I'd better go,' she said. 'I'll email you later?'

He nodded his head without saying anything. She picked up her coat and left.

Rose headed straight back to her grandmother's house. The bus came quickly and she hopped off at her stop feeling odd and ruffled. Joshua's story had unsettled her. The story itself was weird but she was sure that the answer lay in Joshua's mind rather than some supernatural phenomenon. He'd trusted her with his private thoughts and she should have been less sceptical.

She took her keys out but the front door opened before she could reach the lock.

Her grandmother was standing there. She had a serious expression on her face.

'Rose,' she said, standing back and holding the door open.

'Hi,' Rose said.

'Come in.'

'Is something wrong?'

'Rose, I did what you asked . . .'

Rose took her coat off, draping it over her arm. Her grandmother shut the front door.

'I rang Mary Linton School for Girls. Well, I tried and then rang again later today. I only just got through to Martha Harewood an hour so ago.'

Rose remembered that she had asked her to speak to the housemistress about Rachel Bliss. It had gone out of her mind. For the first time in days she hadn't thought about those irritating letters and phone calls.

'Was she OK about it? She knows what Rachel is like. Rachel's had problems a number of times . . .'

'I did speak to her.'

'What did she say?'

Her grandmother was looking pained. Had Martha been brusque with her? Told her to keep out of it?

'Rose, I don't know how to tell you this so I'll just come out with it. This girl, Rachel Bliss, who used to be your friend, well, there's been a terrible accident. She was found dead this morning.'

'What?'

'They found her in the boating lake. Drowned.'

Rose didn't say a word. She stared at her grandmother.

'I'm afraid so. Martha Harewood told me . . .'

'That can't be right.'

'I can see you're upset.'

'But she just wrote to me. There must be a mistake.'

'I'm afraid it is her,' her grandmother said. 'There's no mistake.'

Rose felt weak at the knees. Her grandmother put her hand out to steady her. She could hardly believe it.

Rachel Bliss was dead.

SEVEN

Rose was sitting cross-legged in the studio. Her pad was open in front of her and she was sketching furiously. On the page were three drawings of an eye. One was from the front, another was profiled and the third was closed. It was part of an assignment she was working on, *Windows*. She had pages of sketches of actual windows and cameras and computer screens and keyholes. She was close to pulling together her ideas and submitting her assignment. This was the week to finish it.

She stared at the profiled eye and then made a couple of alterations with her pencil. It was rubbish. She scribbled across it. Then she drew straight hard lines across the others. She tore the page out and screwed it up and tossed it on the floor beside her.

Her back was sore and she wanted to lean against something. The sofa was too far away, though, and it was too much effort to move.

Rachel Bliss dead! How could it be so?

It was gone nine in the evening. She'd spent some time earlier with Anna, who had given her the news about Rachel Bliss as though she was telling her about the death of a close relative. Her grandmother had been very sympathetic and concerned and had asked Rose to tell her about her friendship with Rachel. Rose had summed it up in a few sentences.

She came into our House halfway through term. She didn't have any friends so Martha Harewood asked me and another couple of girls to look after her.

She had the next bedroom to me so I saw a lot of her.

We weren't very friendly at first but then after a while we spent time together.

We fell out last Easter. We weren't friends any more then.

Anna had made a plate of toast for Rose. She spoke quietly and reverently as if Rose was in mourning. She wasn't, though. Far from it. She was simply shocked to the core that Rachel was dead. Anna, who was due to go out for the evening, hovered by the door looking uncertain.

I could stay in, if you want?

I don't have to go. I don't mind keeping you company . . .

I'll cancel my weekend away. I don't want you to be on your own at a time like this . . .

Rose assured her she should go.

Now she was alone, pretending to work on a school assignment. She stretched her legs out and stood up. She stepped across and sat on the sofa, holding her back straight.

Rachel Bliss dead.

It was hard to believe.

How long had they been friends? A year? More?

There were times, during that year, when Rose wondered if their relationship could be called a *friendship* at all.

Some weeks before Easter, in Year Ten, Martha Harewood sent a note for Rose to come and see her. When she arrived there were two other girls there whom she knew, Amanda Larkin and Molly Wallace. This depressed her immediately. Amanda and Molly were *nice* girls who helped the teachers out, who got clubs going, who were always befriending people who were homesick or in trouble. She hoped that Martha was not trying to draw her into some sort of friendship group with them.

The two girls were sitting on Martha's sofa. Rose sat on the floral armchair, hearing the legs creak as they usually did. Martha Harewood pointed to the jug of squash on the coffee table but Rose shook her head.

It was usually a treat to be in Martha's rooms. In the early days, when she first came to the boarding school, Martha had made a fuss of her. It was January, the winter term and her mother had been gone for two and half months. In those days, being a Year Seven, she had had to share her bedroom with two other girls but she hadn't minded. Martha invited her every week to make sure she was all right. She let her sit in the floral armchair and talked to her about things that were happening in the school. She often started with *I shouldn't tell you this but . . .* It made Rose feel special as if she was a friend of Martha's. One day Martha surprised her by pointing out the photo of a young girl of about five that sat on a sideboard. *This was my daughter*, she said. *She died of cancer. So I do know how you feel. I do know what it's like to lose someone.* It had been a startling moment and Rose had realised that she wasn't the only person who carried a huge sorrow around with her.

It made her feel close to Martha and she didn't mind, as the months went by, that the visits became less often. She found her feet and began to feel comfortable around the old school building and wandering the grounds. She made friends; not close, but people to spend time with.

By Year Ten she was an 'old' girl, someone who kept herself to herself but who had a number of girls who she spent time with. She no longer needed a shoulder to cry on. That was why she was surprised when the Housemistress asked her to come and see her.

Martha sat and poured herself a glass of squash.

'Girls, I've asked you here in the hope that you will help me out. We have a new girl joining Eliot House. Her name is Rachel Bliss. She's been in Brontë House since last September and was a friend of poor Juliet Baker. She hasn't really settled since the tragedy so it's been decided that she should move House and join our little family.'

Martha looked at each of them in turn. Rose didn't recognise the name Rachel Bliss. She wasn't in any of her classes.

'What I'm hoping is that you three girls could just look out for Rachel. Show her where everything is, make sure she knows about meal sittings, rules for bathing, prep times and so on. You could introduce her to your friendship groups.'

Amanda and Molly were smiling widely.

'I've put her in Bluebell room.'

Rose looked up. Bluebell was the room next to hers. It had been used for a while by a Chinese girl who had gone back home just before Christmas.

'Are you OK with this?'

'Yes,' Molly said. 'That's no problem. We'll look after her, won't we, Amanda?'

Amanda nodded happily.

'Rose?'

She didn't answer straight away. She hated this kind of situation. She remembered when she'd first started at Mary Linton there were a couple of girls who had clearly been asked to look after her. They always seemed to be around, in the classroom, in the corridor, in the common room, in the queue for food. They were nice girls but Rose didn't connect with them in any way. She was glad when they finally left her alone.

'Rose?'

But Martha was Rose's friend and she had asked for a favour.

'Sure, I'll look out for her.'

'Good. Excellent,' Martha said.

Rachel Bliss arrived late that evening. Rose had left the common room with a headache and had lain down on her bed to read. She heard noises from the room next door just after ten. The door opened and shut several times and she could hear Martha's voice, muffled. There was quiet after a while and Rose listened at the wall. She could hear the sound of music playing softly. It was allowed until eleven. After that people were encouraged to go to bed but earphones could still be used. Rose had occasionally fallen asleep with the sound of her favourite band playing in her ears.

The next morning she came out of her room, Daisy, at exactly the moment that Rachel Bliss came out of Bluebell.

'Hi!' Rose said. 'I'm Rose Smith. Do ask me if there's anything you want to know.'

Rachel Bliss looked sleepy. She had shoulder-length blonde hair and pale skin. Her eyes looked a bit puffy as though she hadn't had a good night's sleep.

'Right, thanks,' Rachel said.

Just then Amanda and Molly appeared at the end of the corridor. Molly let out a squeal and rushed up to Rachel. Rose walked off, glad to be out of the way. After that she saw Rachel Bliss in classes and at mealtimes. She was invariably with Amanda or Molly or some of their friends.

One evening, a couple of weeks after Rachel had arrived, there was a knock on her door. She opened it and found Rachel standing there.

'OK if I come in for five minutes?'

Rose frowned. No one came into her room. It was her private place where she could get away from the constant hum of chatter. She held the door tight.

'Not really, it's a bit messy . . .'

'I wouldn't ask but it's really important.'

Rose pulled the door back and Rachel walked into her room.

'It's not messy at all. You should see mine! Oh my God! You play violin! That's hard. I tried the guitar once but it gave me blisters.'

Rose didn't answer. Her laptop was open on the desk and showed her Facebook page.

'I got so fed up with Facebook!' Rachel said. 'I had over four hundred friends and it was driving me nuts.'

'What do you want?' Rose said, feeling uneasy, not liking her being there.

'Wait,' Rachel said, her finger in the air. 'All will be explained.'

Just then, there was the sound of footsteps in the corridor and voices talking quickly. Rose recognised them as Molly's and Amanda's. They stopped as they got closer. Rose heard a knock on the next room door. She was puzzled. She looked at Rachel but Rachel had her index finger over her lips.

'Rachel?' Amanda called out, knocking again.

'The door's open, look!' Molly said.

'Rachel, are you all right?'

'She definitely said to come at seven.'

'Rachel?'

'Push the door open,' Molly said.

Rose went to speak. She didn't like being a party to this stupid situation but Rachel shook her head decisively.

'There's no one here,' Amanda said.

'No.'

There was silence for a minute.

'Should we wait? She did say she had something important to tell us.'

'No, let's go. Maybe she's in the common room.'

'Yeah, let's try there.'

Footsteps sounded, moving away up the corridor. The girls' voices receded. When it was completely quiet Rose turned to Rachel.

'What was all that about?'

'Those two, they're really sweet and kind but they're driving me insane.'

'You should tell them.'

'I've tried . . . but you know they're so . . .'

'Incorrigible?'

'Relentless, I was going to say. They're like puppy dogs. Lovely, nice but OH! I just want them to leave me alone.'

Rachel reached for the door handle. Then she seemed to notice something. She stepped across Rose's room and picked up a book.

'I loved this book. Have you read her others? I love vampire stories. Isn't it a brilliant idea? That you could stay the same age for ever? I've got some more in this series. Would you like to borrow them?'

Rose gave an uncertain smile.

'Oh, wait! I'm being an annoying puppy dog, aren't I?'

'No, don't be silly.'

'I'll leave you. Now that I've got some peace.'

'Sure . . .' Rose said.

'Great, I'll catch you later.'

The next day Rose sat opposite Rachel in breakfast. Later they walked to their respective classes. That night Rachel showed Rose her books, dozens of them in piles on her floor. Rose smiled at the mess and then sat down cross-legged on the carpet to sort through them in case there were some that she hadn't read.

That was the beginning.

*   *   *

The studio was quiet and Rose looked at her sketch pad to see a blank page. She remembered Rachel Bliss standing in her room saying *I love vampire stories*. Her hair was a gold colour and her eyes the lightest blue. A vampire. That was Rachel. She sucked people dry.

EIGHT

'That's so weird,' Joshua said. 'She *drowned* in the school boating lake.'

'Your school had a boating lake?' Skeggsie said, breaking into a cough.

Rose frowned at Skeggsie. Was that all he could say?

She was standing in Joshua's study, next door to his bedroom. It was a big room with lots of computer equipment. One of the tables had been cleared, though, and on it was *The Butterfly Project*. Alongside it were lined pages of notes as if someone had read it for an essay. Rose saw some pages printed out from websites: **Code Crackers, Morsification, Cipher Plus, Bletchley Code Breakers.** On the other half of the table lay one of the notebooks Joshua had taken from Frank Richards. It was open at the photograph of the Russian man.

'How did you find out? How come you didn't email me?' Joshua said.

'A boating lake!'

Rose stared at Skeggsie with mounting annoyance.

It was 5.30 and she had called in to see them on her way home from school. Although she'd known about Rachel for twenty-four hours she hadn't communicated it to Joshua. They'd left things on an uneven note the previous day with all his talk about *special* feelings and *second sight*. It had felt awkward and it didn't seem the right thing to do to unload further upset on him. Now, looking around his study at the paraphernalia to do with their missing parents, she wished she hadn't mentioned it at all.

'Tell us everything. Sit down.'

There were two chairs in the room and both were covered with the equipment that had been cleared off the table. Neither of them seemed to notice so she remained standing and launched into what had happened, explaining to Skeggsie about the letters and phone calls she'd received from Rachel Bliss. Then she described the things that Rachel had written. When she talked about her seeing the ghost of Juliet Baker she looked away from Joshua, aware that it was an uncomfortable area between them. Finally she reported what Anna had told her.

'That's it!' she said. 'She's dead. Found in the boating lake.'

She leant on the table, her hand next to *The Butterfly Project*.

'That's terrible. I mean, I know you didn't like the girl much but . . .'

'How come you didn't like her?' Skeggsie said, pulling a blue inhaler from his shirt pocket and sucking on it.

'She bullied her,' Joshua said.

'No,' Rose said. 'Not exactly . . .'

'Violence?'

'No.'

'Intimidation?'

'No, not really . . .'

'What then?'

'I can't really explain.'

Skeggsie tutted, rolling his eyes.

'What?' she demanded.

'Girl's stuff, *hurt feelings*.'

'What do you know about it?' she said, instantly irked.

'I know about being bullied,' Skeggsie said slowly, moving towards the table, tidying up some of the printed pages there.

'Just because you had a hard time, that doesn't mean you're some kind of expert on it!'

'I didn't say I was . . .'

'You've got no idea what it was like,' Rose said.

'I had some horrible experiences . . .'

'But not like mine!'

''Course. I was in a boys' school.'

'Don't say you had a harder time than me. Don't say it.'

'Rosie . . .' Joshua said. 'You know Skeggsie had a bad time.'

'But he shouldn't talk like he is in some sort of competition.'

'I'm not.'

'People can get hurt in different ways.'

'I know that.'

'You don't have the monopoly in getting hurt!' she said, her voice loud and scratchy.

Skeggsie turned away and began fiddling with Joshua's keyboard. Rose closed her eyes as a tear slid out.

'I'm sorry,' she said. 'I know you got hurt. Joshua told me. I'm upset about my friend. I was just taking it out on you. I didn't mean that kind of bullying. I'm sorry. It's hard to explain.'

'Let's make some tea,' Joshua said, taking Rose's elbow and leading her out of the room.

The kitchen table was also full of stuff. Rose sat down and pushed away piles of printouts. The name Viktor Baranski was highlighted on a nearby page but she didn't look at it. Her throat was cracked and she was on the brink of crying. Why had she exploded at Skeggsie? Of all people? Skeggsie who had been picked on at school. Then, while at university, he'd had his flat broken into by students who had once been lodgers there. Skeggsie did know about people's cruelty – it was just that he seemed to carry that knowledge with such smugness.

Why did she find it so hard to like him?

Joshua placed a mug of tea in front of her.

'Don't get upset. You know what Skeggsie's like. In any case, his asthma's playing up and it makes him tetchy.'

'I shouldn't have shouted at him . . .'

'It was my fault. I mentioned the dreaded "B" word.'

'He thinks I'm stupid.'

'He likes you. Believe me, I'd know if he didn't. Now do you want to talk about it? Pardon me for saying it but do you think all that emotion was really meant for someone else – not Skeggsie. Is it for this girl who you say you "hated"?'

Joshua made the quotation signs with his fingers.

'You're psychoanalysing me now.'

'Someone has to.'

'Do you charge?'

'A hundred pounds an hour.'

She mustered a smile and drank her tea.

'But there are some cases that are so fascinating I will do them for free.'

'You know what? It's simple. I didn't like her and now she's dead. The complicated bit is that she reached out for me to help her and I ignored it.'

He didn't speak.

'You know if she had been in the water and cried out to me I would have raced over to help her. No matter how she had hurt my feelings. But, because her cries were from a distance, in letters and phone calls, I could just ignore it. God! It was only weeks ago that I stood round while another girl got killed! What sort of person am I?'

'Hey, you're a really good person.'

The door opened behind her and she could feel Skeggsie come in.

'Sorry, Skeggs, again,' she said, without looking round.

''S OK. Any tea going?'

They sat drinking tea and Joshua got out a packet of breadsticks, which they all nibbled their way through. After a while, when she felt better, Rose focused on the printouts on the table. The name Viktor Baranski was highlighted in most of them.

'What's going on with all this stuff? You and Skeggsie look as though you're up to something.'

'Yeah, well, after . . . Well, I thought it was time to get on with the practical side of things. Tell her what we've found out, Skeggs.'

Skeggsie took a deep breath and pulled the pages on the table together.

'We've been looking at the guy whose photo we've got in the notebook. Viktor Baranski. Ex navy. Might have given information to British secret services.'

Rose tried to look interested.

'Baranski was murdered in 2006 and there was a hint of the Russian secret police's involvement, blah, blah. His company fell apart although his son is still in London.

Lev Baranski. Thirty-one years old. He runs a restaurant in South Kensington.'

'So,' said Joshua dramatically, 'Skeggsie and I are going there tomorrow.'

'What for?'

'To see Lev Baranski.'

'Oh.'

'He's the only link we've got to Frank Richards and then to Dad and Kathy. His dad's photograph is in the notebook.'

'What are you going to say to him?'

'Not sure. We'll work out some story when we get there.'

'You're going *undercover*?' Rose said, smiling.

'Sort of,' Joshua said. 'But that's not all we're doing. We're driving up to Norfolk at the weekend. We're going to look for the places marked on Dad's map.'

'You two?' Rose said, looking at each of them.

'Yeah. Skeggs is driving.'

Rose didn't say anything. She hadn't been asked to go along either to the restaurant or to Norfolk. She hadn't been included in these adventures. She should have felt hurt by it but she didn't. She just felt weary.

'You could come!' Joshua said, as if reading her mind.

She shook her head. 'I've got stuff to sort out. Work that's overdue at school. I need, maybe, to spend a bit of time on my own.'

'OK,' Joshua said. 'I'll have my laptop with me and phone, so plenty of ways to stay in touch.'

'Right, you can send me updates of your escapade!'

'It's not an *escapade*, Rosie. This is serious stuff,' Joshua said, looking mildly hurt.

''Course it is,' Rose said.

'And,' Skeggsie said, 'we've started to try and fathom the secret code in the book.'

Rose stood up. Secret codes and escapades. It was like something out of an old-fashioned adventure story. While they were playing around with all this she had the weight of knowledge that someone had asked for her help and she had done nothing. Even if that someone was Rachel Bliss.

She went out into the hall and got her coat and bag.

'See you, guys,' she shouted and headed for the stairs.

On Thursday morning, before getting ready for school, she rang Martha Harewood. Her next phone call was to Joshua. He answered immediately.

'When are you going to Norfolk?' she asked bluntly.

'Tomorrow morning. But there's a slight change of plan. Skeggsie can't come. His asthma's flared up. Temperature, wheezing. He's in bed sucking on his nebuliser.'

'Oh! Is it serious?'

'He's like this every now and again. He just has to drop everything, take the steroids and antibiotics and wait till his peak flow gets better. He should be OK in a few days.'

'Peak flow?' Rose said.

'It's an asthma thing. Not known to us regular people with working lungs.'

'Right.'

'I've seen him like this a lot. Believe me, he'll bounce back.'

'So what about Norfolk?'

'I'm going on my own.'

'How will you get there?'

'Skeggsie says I can take his car.'

'You can drive?'

'Yes, Rosie, I can drive.'

'I didn't know.'

'There's lots you don't know about me.'

'Can I come? I want to go to my old school. I've looked on Google Maps. It's about twelve miles from Stiffkey. That's where you're going, isn't it? You could drop me off. I've spoken to my old housemistress and she says that I can stay there for a couple of nights. You can come back for me on Sunday.'

'What about your gran?'

'She's going away for the weekend.'

'Why are you going to your old school?'

'I want to find out what happened to Rachel. Also I want to give the police some letters that she wrote me. I feel I want to be there, where it happened, even just for a short time.'

'To get it out of your system?'

'Maybe.'

'OK, I'll pick you up tomorrow about nine.'

'Thanks.'

She sat back on her bed, Rachel's letters beside her. The trip would mean missing college the next day but it couldn't be helped. She was finally going back to Mary Linton.

Even though it was too late to do any good.

NINE

Rose sat in the front of Skeggsie's Mini. Her rucksack was on the back seat. She'd packed the minimum of things that she would need: a change of clothes and her laptop. Her mobile was on her knee.

They went at a steady pace, Rose watching Joshua drive the car competently. How could she not have known that he drove? She must have had amazement written all over her face because he glanced at her and started to explain.

'My Uncle Stu taught me to drive,' he said, 'when I was sixteen. He used to take me to this disused airfield that he knew. And he let me drive the car round and round. He sat back and got his tin of tobacco out and made ten roll-ups while I drove. Then, when I was seventeen, he put in for my theory and my test and I passed first time.'

Rose pictured Joshua sitting nervously at the wheel of his uncle's car, driving in circles around an airfield.

'He's mad about cars. He's got this MG Roadster in his garage that he's been renovating for years.'

'Has he been in touch lately?'

'Yes, he's got a girlfriend at long last. Her name's Susie. I think it's *love*. He mentions her in his emails a lot.'

They were heading off the M25 towards the M11 and Joshua swore under his breath when he saw the traffic queuing.

Rose had seen a couple of photos of Stuart in Joshua's study. He didn't look much like his brother, Brendan. He was thinner in the face and had short cropped hair.

'Does he know you're looking for your dad?'

'No.'

'How come?'

'He doesn't really like to talk about Dad much. When I first went to live with him he was all sympathetic and tried to cheer me up but as time went on it was difficult to keep the conversation going. There's only so many times you can ask someone what their childhood memories of their brother are. I'd say something like, *When you and Dad were teenagers did you go out together?* And he'd say, *Me and Bren went out a few times.* Or I might say, *What was Dad like when he was my age?* and he'd say. *Our Bren was all right.* Stu isn't talkative. He's the silent type. The truth is, if I'd stayed living with him, I wouldn't be looking for Dad. It's being with Skeggsie that made me properly look for Dad.'

'Why?'

'Because I'm at a distance. Nothing I can do can hurt

Stu's feelings. And then there's all the web stuff that I could never have done without Skeggs.'

'How is he today?'

'So, so. Coughing a lot. He's taking the steroids. It'll take a couple of days for those to kick in.'

'Don't. You're making me feel sorry for Skeggsie and I don't want to do that.'

'You still don't like him?'

'Making my mind up.'

'Maybe he's a bit like you? Maybe that's why you find it hard to get along with him.'

'No!' she said. 'He's nothing like me. Nothing at all!'

'OK.'

They drove on, the conversation stalling, following the signs for Cambridge. Joshua tried the radio, flicking between stations. Rose pulled a pile of CDs from the door pocket and began to look through them. She was pleasantly surprised. Skeggsie's taste in music wasn't as bad as she feared.

'You know that restaurant owned by the son of Viktor Baranski? In South Kensington? I went to it.'

'Yeah?' she said.

Even though Skeggsie was unwell Joshua had still gone.

'It's close to South Ken station on the way to the museums. It's a street which is full of coffee bars and cafes. This restaurant is called Eastern Fare.'

'Is it a Russian restaurant?'

Joshua was heading off the motorway at a turning marked for Norwich.

'Not really. It's got Russian signs everywhere but it just serves coffee and sandwiches and hot lunches. It looks a bit run-down. We had a sandwich and coffee.'

She frowned. 'I thought you went on your own?'

'No, someone from uni came with me. That girl you saw last week, Clara.'

Rose stared straight ahead. Clara, the girl with the yellow hair.

'I did get to talk to Lev Baranski! It was a lot easier than I expected. In the end I just asked him for a job.'

'A job?' she said quietly.

'Yes. I saw this guy at a table at the back of the cafe working at a laptop so I just went up to him and I said, *Excuse me, are you Mr Baranski?* And he looked up and said, *Who wants to know?* I said, *I'm looking for a job as a waiter and someone down the street said I should try here. He thought you might need help. I'm a student and I'm just looking for part-time work.* There was this long silence and I couldn't tell what he was thinking. His face was completely flat, no hint of expression. He was youngish but dressed old, in a suit and tie. He called this other guy over, Mikey. He said, *This lad is looking for a job.* Mikey said, in this heavy Russian accent, *We don't have jobs now.* Lev then said, *Leave your details with Mikey and we'll let you know if anything comes up.* So I left a fake name, then me and Clara left.'

Rose had an image of Joshua and Clara leaving the restaurant. Joshua was holding the door open for Clara and she was laughing up at him, both of them thrilled with their little plan. Rose could see Clara's hair snaking over her shoulders. In her mind it was longer and thicker than before, the kind of hair that could be gathered up into a scrunchie and pinned up on the back of her head. Rose grabbed hold of a strand of her own hair and pulled it along her chin. She turned away and leant her head against the glass.

'It's a start, seeing Lev Baranski. I don't know whether he is important or not but every little bit of information needs to be followed up,' Joshua said.

'Um.'

They passed a sign for Mildenhall. She was beginning to recognise the road. She'd done the journey many times with Anna at the beginning and end of each term. There would be a roundabout and they would go off to the second left and go past the Lakenheath Air Base. It was a journey she'd usually done with pleasure, keen to get back to school after spending too much time alone with Anna. The last time she did it, just after Easter, she'd done it with a heavy heart. She was no longer friends with Rachel Bliss and had only dragged herself back to school to take her exams.

Now she was gloomy because Joshua had a new friend or perhaps even a *girlfriend*. Her feelings for him were muddling up her thoughts.

'I might just close my eyes for a while. I didn't sleep that well last night,' she said, not wanting to talk any more.

'Use my jacket as a pillow.'

She leant over the back seat and picked up Joshua's jacket and folded it in half so that it was bulky. She fitted it between her face and the window and closed her eyes. She heard music come on and after a while she heard Joshua singing, quietly.

She didn't sleep, though; just kept her eyes closed, cross with her reaction to the mention of Clara. With everything else going on how could the existence of this girl make her feel worse? Rachel Bliss was dead. Wasn't that what she should be thinking about?

They drove for what seemed like a long time. They stopped once at a petrol station and Rose got out to use the toilet. When she came out Joshua was standing by the car with drinks and doughnuts. They ate and drank and then went on their way. The traffic shot past and she saw a sign for King's Lynn. Soon after that they passed Fakenham and she knew then that it wasn't far to go. She sat up, making a show of stretching her arms as if she had dropped off to sleep again.

'Nearly there, Rosie,' Joshua said chirpily.

'Where are you staying?' she said.

'There's an inn in Stiffkey. I've booked a room for two nights. It'll give me enough time to scout about, talk to some people.'

But what do you think you'll achieve? What are you actually looking for? Is there any point following markings on a map that probably have nothing to do with anything?

Rose wanted to say these things but she didn't.

'What about you? Where will you sleep?'

'There are always spare rooms in school. Oh, look. The entrance is a mile or so on. Just drop me at the gates. I'll walk down the drive myself. I could do with stretching my legs.'

'I'll come by after lunch on Sunday, say two, and pick you up.'

'Pick me up at the same place. Don't bother to come down to the school.'

'Why? You ashamed of me?'

''Course not,' she said, as the car pulled over on to the grass verge just before the entrance gates of Mary Linton School for Girls.

'You've got your laptop? And your phone? I'll send you messages. Let you know what I'm doing. You could send me messages as well, tell me what's happening about your friend's death.'

She nodded. She opened the passenger door and got out.

Joshua did the same. She pulled on her coat and, pushing the seat forward, she leant in to get her rucksack out of the back. When she was standing by the car Joshua came over beside her.

'Take care,' he said, leaning down to kiss her on the cheek.

She felt his lips on her skin and closed her eyes for a split second.

Then he was gone and she turned and went through the gates of Mary Linton School for Girls, the sound of the Mini pulling away behind her.

TEN

The school building came into view after she'd been walking for about ten minutes. It was the colour of autumn, rust red and stood four storeys high, looking like a large country house. There were newer buildings attached to the side and back but these were mostly veiled with trees. The windows on the three lower floors were imposing, almost floor to ceiling, but on the fourth floor, where some of the sleeping areas were, there were dormer windows.

She glanced over to the right. In the near distance she could see the lake and the boathouse. She quickened her step. Her bag was feeling heavy and although it was a grey cold day she was hot. She stopped for a moment and slipped her coat off, folding it over her arm.

There was hardly anyone around even though it was just before one o'clock. At 1.15 the lunch bell would go and then the place would become busy. She was feeling hungry herself but it would be strange to go into the dining hall again, to queue up with a tray in hand and walk along the counter selecting her lunch. She thought she'd finished with all that. During those last weeks in the school when she'd taken her exams she'd counted the days until she could pack her stuff and go to live in Anna's house. Standing in front of the salad bar, her eye flicking across the giant bowls of coleslaw, bean salad and lettuce, she'd imagined making a single portion of food for herself. She'd use small pots and pans, chop up tiny bunches of herbs, slice half an onion and a couple of tomatoes. She'd pick up a handful of dried pasta only. Just enough for her; it would be luxurious.

But just now she was hungry and would enjoy some salad and lasagne or quiche, a portion of garlic bread on the side.

She walked through the main school car park and towards the quad, a small area of benches and rose bushes and gravel where students were allowed to sit quietly and talk or read or listen to iPods. She stopped for a second and glanced up at the windows at the very top of the building. At the corner was her old room, Daisy. To the left of it was Rachel's room, Bluebell.

It was here that Rachel said she'd looked up and seen the face of Juliet Baker in her room. Rose stared at the window for a moment, then she swivelled round and looked in the opposite direction at the line of trees that edged the car park. That was where Rachel had seen the ghost at night, its face bright amid the darkness.

She made a *tsk* sound and carried on. What was it that Rachel had seen? Something real? Or something conjured up out of her own imagination?

Rose walked on. She stepped inside the building and went up to the receptionist. It was someone she didn't recognise, someone new. She gave her name and the woman looked at a printout and then gave her a visitor's badge. Ten minutes later Rose had walked up the four flights of stairs and was standing on the landing next to a sign that said *Eliot House*.

The bell went then for lunch recess.

In the distance doors began to open and shut and there was the sound of students moving around on the floors below. There was no talking, just the sound of feet shuffling, stamping, sliding along the wood floors, moving towards the outside of the building where the students would head for the refectory.

She went past the sign for *Eliot House*.

It was part of the fourth floor of the building and it housed the students who were members of the House named after George Eliot. Eliot House students were the only ones who slept and lived in the original school building. It consisted of dormitories and shared and single rooms. It had bathrooms and a shower block and two small kitchens. There was a large common room full of armchairs and beanbags with a big television and table tennis tables.

When Rose was a student in the school she could recognise all of the Eliot House girls and not just because of the small badges they wore. She knew twenty or so to talk to and a couple who were people she spent time with. Her closest friend in four and a half years had been Rachel Bliss.

She walked along the main corridor and was heading for Martha Harewood's room when she heard footsteps coming up the stairs from behind. She stopped and waited. Amanda Larkin turned on to the corridor and broke into a smile when she saw her.

'Rose! It's good to see you. Oh! I'll bet you've come back because of Rachel Bliss? Horrible business.'

Rose nodded. 'Horrible. She wrote me some letters . . .'

'Did she?'

'I brought them to give to the police.'

'They were here today.'

'Where's Molly?'

'She's around somewhere.'

'I was just going to see Martha.'

'I wouldn't,' she said. 'She is in a real state. She looks as though she's going to burst into tears every time she comes out of her rooms.'

'Oh . . .'

Amanda put her hand lightly on Rose's shoulder.

'I'm just getting something from my room, then I'm going to lunch. Come with me. See some of the others. Have something to eat. See Martha later.'

'My bag . . .' Rose said.

'Put it in my room. And your coat. You can pick them up at the end of lunch.'

Rose handed over her stuff and allowed herself to be guided down the stairs and out of the building towards the refectory. After saying hello to many girls and after some elbowing and queuing, she found herself sitting at one of the window tables used by the older years. People were looking at her. The girl dressed in black and white among the different shades of green. Since leaving she'd been in touch with some of these girls on Facebook but it had always been general chatter, nothing personal. It was hot and she pushed her sleeve up and the girls closest to her gasped at her deep blue butterfly tattoo. She ignored their looks and concentrated on her plate, tucking into her lasagne and salad. It tasted good and eating it slowly gave her a chance to just sit and listen to the conversation around her. Her presence had sparked off discussions about Rachel Bliss's death.

'It was terrible, Rose. I was up early and heard this shouting coming from outside. I looked out of my window. My room's got a good view of the boating lake. I saw the head groundsman running across the grass shouting.'

'He discovered her. That must have been a fright! He was going to check the boathouse and saw her floating on the water by the jetty. Face down!'

'I heard he got into the water and pulled her out.'

'No, no, it wasn't him it was one of the gardeners. He was going to try and bring her back to life.'

'Mouth to mouth. You know when they breathe into someone's lungs? Resuscitation?'

'People have lived in water for hours. Oh my God, I've seen it. Their body closes down. It was on a TV programme. You could be dead for hours, then they can bring you back to life.'

'Don't be pathetic!'

'Anyway, he pulled her out and tried to save her life but it didn't work.'

'Her clothes pulled her down. She was wearing coat, boots, the lot.'

'It was the middle of the night. Freezing cold!'

'I heard they found a bottle of vodka in the water.'

Rose listened to them. Girls she'd known for three and a half years. They talked in a shocked way but there was also an undertone of excitement. Something dramatic had happened. It was something to talk about, to chew over, to interpret.

'If it turns out that Rachel was drunk it will be bad publicity for the school.'

'Don't say that! What's that got to do with anything?'

'I liked Rachel.'

'You were one of the few.'

'That's not true. She was Rose's friend for a while.'

'Rose saw through her. Everyone did eventually.'

'Apart from Molly.'

Rose pushed her plate away and stood up. *Rachel was drunk?*

'Good to see you, Rose. Great tattoo. I'm having one after my exams . . .'

Amanda followed her as she walked through the diners towards the exit.

'You're not upset, are you, Rose?' Amanda said.

'No. Though I didn't know the details before so I didn't have any pictures in my head. Now I do.'

'No one knows what really happened. It's all just gossip.'

'I'll see Martha and put my things in my room.'

Just then Molly appeared at the door. She gave a half-smile when she saw Rose and walked towards them.

'I heard you'd come back. You look great, Rose, doesn't she, Amanda?'

'We're just going to my room to get Rose's things. Are you feeling a bit better?'

Molly nodded.

'She's been really upset about Rachel. They've been quite friendly this term.'

Rose was surprised. She never would have thought of *Molly* as a friend of Rachel's.

'We spent some time together. I liked her . . .' Molly's voice broke and she dragged a large handkerchief out of her sleeve.

'Oh, Molly,' Amanda said.

'I'm all right,' she said, blowing her nose. 'I'll see you later.'

Molly walked off towards the tables.

'Come to my room after dinner if you want!' Amanda called after her.

'Will she be all right?' Rose said.

'She's been like this ever since it happened. Inconsolable.'

They walked across the grass. Over to the left was the lake. Rose paused and so did Amanda. The lake took up a huge chunk of the grounds and some years before some of it had been reclaimed to make the playing fields bigger. At the same time the lake and the boathouse were renovated. Rose remembered the diggers and the pipes and the workmen who had been around for months when she first came to Mary Linton. Then one day the lake was smaller but deeper and with several ornamental features, a small island and a number of inlets at the periphery. The boathouse had been rebuilt with a jetty branching out from it into the water. It was long enough to moor a dozen or more rowing boats and canoes which the girls used in the spring and summer months. On one side of the jetty was a slate wall which meant that girls could queue up and wait for the boats without any fear of falling off.

Rose had a sudden memory. Rachel and her sitting on

the jetty on a summer's evening, their legs dangling, their toes touching the surface of the water. Rachel taking out a can of insect repellent and spraying it over both of them.

'Do they know *when* she went into the water?' Rose said, frowning.

'In the night sometime? Or early morning? No one's told us. I didn't see her get pulled out. Only a handful of girls saw and as soon as the staff knew they marched them back to the building.'

'Why would she go out to the lake? At night?'

'People did. They do. It's forbidden to go out of the building after lights out but people do it.'

'OK in June. But November?'

Amanda shrugged.

'The girls are right about one thing. It'll be terrible publicity for the school. First Juliet Baker. Now this.'

Rose nodded. As they walked back in the direction of the main school she thought of Juliet Baker and remembered the things that Rachel had said in her letter about seeing her *ghost*. It made her feel uncomfortable for a moment because she herself had thought she'd seen her mother three times after she vanished. Twice in the school car park and once in the sickbay. At the time she had never said the word *ghost* to herself but maybe it had been there, in her consciousness. Now, since she'd found out that her mother was still alive, she wondered whether those sightings had in fact been real. Her mother checking up on her; making sure, from a distance, that she was all right. Rose liked this thought.

They walked up the stairs back to Eliot House.

'How come Molly was friends with Rachel?'

'They just began to hang round together.'

'But I thought you and she were best friends.'

'Not for a long time, Rose. Not since the beginning of Year Eleven. We sort of drifted apart.'

'I didn't know. I never noticed.'

'No, you were always too hung up with Rachel to notice anyone else.'

Rose felt the rebuke. She tried to think of an answer but couldn't. She walked on in silence until they got to Amanda's room. She picked up her coat and bag.

'I'm going into Holt in the morning. I thought I'd take Molly. Try and cheer her up a bit. Why not come along?'

'I might. I'll let you know.'

She heard Amanda's footsteps fading down the stairwell.

Too hung up with Rachel to notice anyone else.

The words stung her and she wondered if perhaps Amanda was right. Another girl, a few weeks before, had said that Rose was aloof, not interested in other people. She had been a student at her new high school in London. Had it been true at Mary Linton as well?

She walked in the direction of Martha Harewood's rooms. She knocked on the door as she had done so many times. In the past there had always been a couple of seconds, wait and then she would hear Martha's voice singing out the words, *Come in!* But this time there was just silence so she knocked again and then moments later the door was open and Martha appeared.

'Rose,' she said, with a shaky smile. 'Come in.'

She followed Martha into her sitting room. Martha went across to her desk. It was packed full of things and she seemed to be shuffling from one sheet of paper to the next in a distracted way. Her shoulders were rounded and her voice a little indistinct.

'I've put you in your old room. It's not been used since you left. Actually, quite a few beds have not been used what with the financial downturn. Not so many people sending their daughters to a private boarding school these days!'

She turned round.

'Do sit down, Rose.'

Rose sat down.

'We've had a most terrible time here. To lose a young girl, like this. It's just dreadful,' Martha said.

'You know Rachel wrote to me?' Rose said after a few moments.

Martha nodded. 'Your grandmother mentioned something when she rang.'

'I've brought the letters with me. I thought the police might want to see them. Would *you* like to see them? They're here in my bag.'

Martha Harewood shook her head.

'Best to pass them on to the police. Mrs Abbott is liaising with them. I believe they're due into school again tomorrow.'

'How was Rachel? How was she since . . .'

'Since you left? She seemed a bit lost. Her behaviour improved for a while but then I found alcohol in her room a couple of times and I had to write home. That was difficult.'

'I heard she was friends with Molly Larkin.'

'Yes. An odd combination. I think it probably wasn't the first choice for either of them. On the other hand I've seen all sorts of girls make good long friendships in unpromising circumstances. I had my hopes . . .'

'In the letters she seemed very depressed. She kept mentioning Juliet Baker.'

'Poor Juliet.'

Martha shook her head. She started to speak but the bell for the end of lunchtime went and she looked away from Rose, towards the sound.

'Afternoon classes,' she said.

'I'll go,' Rose said.

'You know where your room is,' Martha said, with a half-smile.

Rose nodded. At the door she heard Martha's voice from behind her.

'You know, Rose, Rachel was a difficult girl but I still cared for her as much as I cared for any of you.'

Rose turned back and was startled to see that Martha's eyes were glittering with tears. Rose's hand moved out as though to offer comfort but Martha shooed it away. She pulled a handkerchief from a pocket and folded it in half and then pressed it to her eyelids.

'I'll see you later,' Rose said.

She walked along the corridor feeling unhappy, her footsteps heavy. Coming up to the room, Daisy, she paused. Adjacent to it was Bluebell, Rachel's room. She dragged her eyes away and opened her own door. The room was exactly the same as it had been on the day she left. The bed against the wall, the desk and chest of drawers opposite. Above the headboard was a cork notice board. It had been the place to pin pictures of bands or movie stars that she liked. Somewhere to put notes and flyers, articles cut out of magazines. Other girls had photographs of their family there, pinned haphazardly, one image overlapping another, some photos literally covering others, a kind of pictorial palimpsest. Rose had had no photos. The pictures she had of her mother she had kept in a drawer.

Now the cork board was blank save for a rash of pin-holes.

She put her rucksack on the bed and sat down beside it.

Everything was the same.

It was as if she had gone back in time.

ELEVEN

After handing Rachel's letters to Mrs Abbott, the head teacher, Rose went outside for a walk in the school grounds. She chose a path that was out of view of the main building. She headed away from the lake towards Ravenswood. The small wood was on the periphery of the Mary Linton grounds. She quickened her step. Five minutes later she was surrounded by trees and bushes.

It was a place much used by girls in their free time. There were signs of them everywhere. Names and initials had been carved into trees even though it was frowned upon. There were rope swings and dens that had been made and discarded. There were clearings where the ground was trodden down and logs had been dragged together for makeshift seats. The wood was big enough to have quiet shaded places where it was possible to find some privacy.

Rose walked for a few minutes and headed for the north end of the wood where there was a clump of birch trees and a giant oak. Beyond this were hedges and fields. On the ground was the husk of an old tree trunk. The first summer she and Rachel became friends they went there. They would sit on the trunk and talk quietly, their voices soft, church-like. They no longer read the vampire books but the wood, even in the daytime, seemed an eerie place. Sometimes the quiet would explode into sound as black crows cawed and croaked. Startled, they'd burst into frightened giggles. Mostly, though, the quiet was disturbed by younger students playing loud games and they'd shoo them off back to their own part of the wood until they were alone again.

During these times they talked. Rachel told Rose about her life.

'Mum and Dad split up a couple of years ago. Dad's got a new wife, Melanie, who's, like, only a few years older than me! She's always giving me stuff and then I have to lie about it. Dad's got this new flat by the Thames. Him and Melanie are always having dinner parties. I help Melanie with the food and she gives me a fifty-pound note. No kidding. A fifty-pound note. When I get home I have to pretend I've had a horrible time and the worse thing is – and this is really bad – my mum's started seeing this guy, Robert? And he's always around and he's got this way of looking at me, as if he's, like, more interested in me than my mum.'

'You should tell her!'

'Trouble is she's so pleased with herself. You don't how much she cried when my dad left. Like, I'd ring up every night and she couldn't speak because she was crying so much. Week after week. I gave up phoning her in the end. I'm *glad* she's got Robert. And it's not like I'm there a lot. In the holidays I just make sure my door's locked at night and the bathroom.'

'Poor Rachel,' Rose said.

Another day Rachel told her about Juliet Baker.

'We were friends. Me and Juliet and Tania. We hung around together. It was really great having her as a friend. She didn't board so, me and Tania, we used to go to her house at weekends. Her mum would make us tea and we'd hang out in her room. She made these cupcakes. They were awesome, with silver balls and decorations on them. And Juliet had a brother. And Tania totally fell for him. She was just in love and every time he came into the room she went scarlet. It was really funny.'

Rose didn't smile because Rachel's voice was cracking.

'I'm really sorry for you. Losing your friend like that.'

'Tania just cried for days. Our housemistress, Joan, she called the doctor in twice, then Tania had to go home for a couple of weeks to get over it. It was the worst time ever.'

'How did you hear about it?'

'Joan came to my room and told me. She said there'd been a terrible accident and that poor Juliet was dead.'

'An accident?'

'They say *accident* because she didn't leave a note so it wasn't completely clear what her intention was. But they found her hanging from a beam in the garage so I think her intention was pretty clear.'

'It must have been terrible.'

'It was.'

Eventually Rose told Rachel about her mother. None of the students in school knew her background. Everyone thought that Rose had been orphaned and lived with her grandmother. It was the truth but it didn't tell the whole story. One afternoon, after they'd been friends for some weeks, Rose started to talk about it.

'No one knows,' she said, after explaining about the disappearance of her mother and Brendan. 'I mean, the staff know but I didn't want any of the students to know so you mustn't say anything.'

'I wouldn't,' Rachel said, shaking her head.

'They've been gone for three and a half years. The fourth of November. The night before Guy Fawkes night. They just vanished. No one really knows what happened to them.'

'So they could be alive,' Rachel said, putting her hand on Rose's arm, rubbing it in a sympathetic way.

Rose nodded. She so much wanted them to be alive.

'There could be a good reason why they've gone into hiding. Maybe their lives were threatened?'

'But why would they just leave us? Without a word?'

'I don't know. How awful for you.'

'You won't say anything to anyone? I just don't want it to be public knowledge. I don't want everyone gossiping about me.'

''Course not. I wouldn't. Anyway, you're my best friend now. Who else would I tell?'

They were best friends. Rose was happy for the first time in years.

Now, in the winter, the wood was not so private. The trees had lost their leaves and Rose could see through them. Across the school grounds was the edge of the lake and the boathouse. She walked out of the wood and headed towards them. It was another place that Rose and Rachel would go and sit. Loads of girls went there on fine evenings and at weekends. Neither Rose nor Rachel ever used the boats, though – they just draped themselves on the jetty or sat in little nooks round the edge of the lake. They rolled their eyes at girls who struggled with the oars or the paddles. They preferred to use the place as a background to their conversations. Even when it was cold and the boats were put away for the winter, they and a few other hardy girls still used it. The wall that edged one side of the jetty acted as a kind of windbreak.

Rose kept to the perimeter of the grounds and took her time. She remembered the night by the boathouse when Rachel first told her about her half-sister, Megan.

* * *

Rose and Rachel had been friends for the summer term and it was only a week until they broke up for the holidays. Things had become a little frosty between them. They'd rowed because Rose had asked Rachel to stop researching her mother's disappearance. Over the days and weeks that followed Rachel had become withdrawn and moody. She wasn't always where she'd said she would be and Rose would find her talking to girls they hardly knew or sitting by herself staring into space. They made arrangements to meet after Rose's violin lessons or badminton but Rachel often wouldn't turn up. Rose was beginning to feel that she'd done something wrong.

The closeness of the holidays made Rose more anxious. They wouldn't see each other for ages. In just over a week she would go to her grandmother's house for the summer. Rachel was going to France with her father and Melanie for two weeks and then away with her mother for the rest. She would be able to contact her by email but still it was a long break.

Rose wondered if Rachel wanted to break up their friendship. Now that Rose no longer wanted to talk about her *tragic past* she thought that Rachel might be bored with her.

It was past nine o'clock in the evening and one of the *Harry Potter* films was being shown in the main hall and girls from all houses were watching. Rose couldn't see Rachel anywhere and she slipped away from the film to find her. After looking in the common room and going back to Rachel's room and finding it empty, she stood by the window and saw a couple of girls standing near the boathouse. One of them was Tania Miller, Rachel's old friend from Brontë House. Rose went down the stairs and headed for the lake. On the way there she saw Tania was walking towards her.

The girl had long brown hair which had a perfect middle parting and hung down each side of her face. It shone as if someone had actually polished it. Tonight she had plaited a strand of it and pulled it back with a grip.

'You looking for Rachel?' Tania said. 'She's round the back.'

Rose watched Tania walk away. She wondered what Rachel was doing with her. They hadn't spent any time together that she'd been aware of, not since Rachel joined Eliot House. She walked round the boathouse to the side that was hidden from the main building. Rachel was sitting, leaning against the wall, with a cigarette in her hand. Rose was surprised. Rachel had said that she'd stopped smoking months before.

'Where've you been? I've been looking for you.'

'Here.'

'You didn't say you were coming here. How come Tania Miller was here?'

'What is this? The third degree? Do I have to ask your permission to speak to Tania?'

'No, I didn't mean that.'

'Well, what then?'

'I just wondered where you were. That's all.'

'Sit down,' Rachel said, patting the grass beside her.

'How come you're smoking?'

'I've got a lot on my mind at the moment.'

'What?'

It suddenly dawned on Rose that maybe Rachel was worried about the holidays. She would have to spend time with her mum's new boyfriend. It was one thing avoiding him now and then but three weeks was a long time for her to keep her bedroom door locked. Maybe this was the very thing that had been making Rachel feel a bit off. The closer they'd got to the holidays the more moody she had become. She was about to say it when Rachel said something that shocked her.

'My half-sister's got leukaemia.'

'What?'

'Melanie's daughter, Megan. She's got leukaemia. She's been having all this treatment and her hair has fallen out. She's been really sick and . . .'

'I didn't know you had a half-sister. You never said!'

'Yeah, well, it's a painful thing to talk about.'

'I'm so sorry!'

'She's not going to die or anything. There's loads of treatments they can use, drugs and stuff.'

Rachel stubbed her cigarette out on the ground. Rose

moved a bit closer to her. She put her arm around Rachel's shoulder.

'What a terrible thing. How old is she?'

'Six, nearly seven. Seven in September.'

'Poor little mite.'

'Yeah, well. It's just one of those things and nothing I can do or say will change it.'

'You should have told me.'

Rachel shrugged. They sat for a while then Rachel stood up, brushing the grass off her legs. She took a last puff of the cigarette and then chucked it into the lake.

'Let's catch the end of *Harry Potter*,' she said. 'It'll take my mind off . . .'

'Yeah, let's.'

Five minutes later they slipped into the back of the hall and watched the last half hour of the film. From time to time Rose turned and looked at Rachel's profile. Her face showed no emotion. She wondered how it felt to know her half-sister was so ill. Why hadn't she told her? Was it that Rose was so full of her own problems that Rachel had had no space to unload her worries about her little sister?

A few days later Rose went on a last-minute shopping trip to Holt with some other girls. While she was there she got a text from Rachel. **Had to go home a couple of days early. No time to say goodbye. See you in September XXX Rachel.**

She made a *tsk* sound. Getting back to school she ran up to Eliot House and found Rachel's room quiet. Most of her stuff was still there but some things had gone. Her bedside table where she kept her make-up, phone, iPod and other personal stuff was clear. Rose was perplexed. In her bag she had a present that she had bought for Rachel. The news about her half-sister had made Rose realise that Rachel was going home to an unhappy situation and she wanted to cheer her up. She'd bought her a silver locket on a chain. She'd found it in an antique shop in Holt. It had cost twenty pounds and was light and pretty. Rose was sure that Rachel would like it but now she had gone and Rose hadn't had a chance to give it to her. She wondered what had happened. Most likely her dad or mum had turned up unannounced and said that Rachel should come now. No doubt they had had to pay extra for Rachel's stuff to be packed by the household staff and sent on at the end of term.

Later, in the refectory, when she'd finished eating, she thought of something. Had Rachel gone home early because of Megan? Had Megan's condition worsened? Was it a family emergency?

It was the only thing that explained her sudden departure.

Just then Tania Miller walked past and caught her eye.

'Tania,' she called.

Tania turned round. She hooked her hair behind her ears and stepped across to Rose's table.

'Did you know that Rachel's gone home early?'

Tania shrugged. 'News to me.'

'She has. I think it might be because of her half-sister, Megan. Did she mention her to you?'

'What? Her half-sister?' Tania's face broke into a grin.

'I thought, maybe, she'd gone because the illness had got worse.'

Tania was shaking her head, her face cracked with an unpleasant smile. She pulled a chair out and sat down.

'Rose, isn't it?' she said, pointing a finger at her.

Rose nodded.

'Rachel doesn't have a half-sister.'

'She told me . . .'

'You can't always believe what Rachel says. She makes some things up.'

A call came from across the hall. Tania looked round and waved at someone.

'Look, Rachel's all right but just don't believe everything she says,' she said and got up and walked away.

Rose felt her face flaming. She shoved her hand in her pocket to get her phone out and felt the paper bag there. She pulled it out. Inside was the locket that she had bought for Rachel. The paper was all screwed up and she tried to smooth it out with the side of her hand. She glanced across at Tania Miller, who was standing talking to a group of girls. One of them looked over in her direction and she wondered whether Tania was telling them about how Rachel had lied to her new friend.

Rose stood up, her throat burning, as she walked back to her room. She went in and sat on her bed. She let the bag with the locket drop on to her duvet. *You can't always believe what Rachel says.* Was there any way she could have misunderstood Rachel? There was not. She knew what Rachel had told her, she could remember the words clearly. *My half-sister has leukaemia.*

Why did she say that?

Why?

Rose lay down. There was a feeling of hurt turning in her chest. Rachel had lied to her, deliberately. She misled her, made her make a fool of herself in front of Tania Miller. Not just that, but she elicited sympathy from Rose for something that didn't exist. Rose, who had a weight of sorrow of her own, had taken time to *feel* something for Rachel.

And it was all a lie.

Rose stood up, too angry to stay where she was. She walked up and down her room, her throat tight with temper. It was over. Her friendship with Rachel Bliss was over.

She would have nothing more to do with her.

Rose arrived at the boathouse. She walked around it until she got to the jetty. It stretched out into the water like a long finger. She walked along it, her footsteps sounding on the wood as she went. It always had a deserted look in the winter months; no boats nestled up beside it; only a handful of girls in hats and scarves and gloves, making a getaway from the central heating and busyness of the buildings. She got to the end of the jetty and stood still for a moment, staring down into the water. It was rippled with a breeze, the grasses at the edge all blowing in one direction.

Rachel's body had been found around here. One of the gardeners got in and tried to pull her out but her clothes were saturated. He needed help to pull her free of the water. A picture came into her head. Two men struggling with the inert body, water running from it, soaked fabric heavy on the wood, a dead weight.

It was too late for resuscitation.

Rachel had probably been dead for hours.

Rose sighed. Rachel had been dead to her for a lot longer.

TWELVE

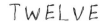

On Saturday morning Rose decided she would go into Holt with Amanda and Molly.

She checked her laptop and found she had two emails from Joshua. The first one had been sent at six the previous day.

I'm in the hotel, the White Rose. I've had a quick look around the village and tried to find some of the places on the map. Tomorrow I'll make a fresh start. Hope things are OK at your old school. Josh XXX

The second one came later at just before eleven.

I've just been talking to some guys in the bar. I showed them Dad's map. They told me that the places marked by Dad are away from the village towards the sea, along the mudflats. There's a path that stretches all along the coast from King's Lynn to Cromer. These mudflats come between the sea and the towns. They're so wide that in most places you can't actually see the sea. Do you remember that I told you about that odd feeling I got?

That the place I was seeing in my head smelled of the sea but wasn't near it? I know you were sceptical but maybe this is the place. Let you know tomorrow. Josh XXX

She sent an answer.

I know a few more details about what happened to Rachel. She went into the lake some time late on Monday evening. Some of the girls say that she'd been drinking so it could be just an accident. Mrs Abbott, my old head teacher, came to see me last night and said that the police were pleased that I'd brought the letters and that they showed Rachel's state of mind in the days before she died. This afternoon, the police want to speak to me (as well as to some of the other students). Keep in touch xxxx Rose

Holt was a town about five miles away from the school. Getting there involved a walk of about a mile and a half to the bus stop. Then it was a five-minute ride.

Amanda was talkative but Molly was quiet. She stared out of the window, a large white handkerchief bunched up in her hand. Amanda talked about how things had been in school that term. Rose listened and nodded but really her mind couldn't latch on to the small talk. She looked at Molly during a quiet moment. Molly always seemed younger than her years. When Rose first knew her she was an excitable character, a bit annoying but good-hearted. Amanda had been like that too but now Amanda seemed years older than Molly. It was as if Molly had stayed in Year Eight, always rushing here and there, her hand up first in class to answer a question. Even the way she dressed was young, wearing odd things in her hair and an old-fashioned mix of childish jumpers and blouses. Today she had a vivid pink feather slide in her hair which looked a little bizarre. Not that Rose was one to comment on other people's clothes but it all added up to the fact that Molly hadn't really grown up yet. It made perfect sense that Amanda and she had drifted apart. The fact that Rachel had befriended her gave Rose an uncomfortable feeling. Rachel had called her a *puppy dog* and Rose remembered Rachel rolling her eyes at Molly on many occasions.

The bus stopped in town and Rose got off, looking round to see the familiarity of the Georgian town with its old-fashioned High Street, its war memorial and numerous tea shops and antique shops for holidaymakers and weekenders. She'd always liked going into Holt. A lot of the other girls preferred to go to the nearby station of Little Radleigh and spend their free time in Norwich. She'd gone a couple of times in Year Ten but in Year Eleven, after she and Rachel had become friends again, the two of them preferred Holt. They dawdled in shops browsing endlessly; antiques, collectables, fashion boutiques and charity shops. Nobody seemed to mind and there was a brilliant arts and crafts area at the back of the High Street where she loved to buy sketch pads.

'Are you going anywhere in particular?' Rose said.

'Library,' Amanda said. 'And Molly's going to come with me to look at some of the vintage clothes shops.'

'Text me when you've finished and we can get a drink.'

'Yeah,' Amanda said.

Rose watched them walk off, Molly a little ahead of Amanda. When they had gone she looked around. It was busy. Holt was always full of people at the weekends. Even in the winter families from London came and stayed in the second homes and shopped in the quaint grocers and bakers. She and Rachel used to make fun of them.

It was cold so Rose walked towards the back of the town in the direction of the Antique and Collectables Emporium, a rickety old building which covered two floors. Upstairs was a huge room full of stripped wooden tables and chairs and a variety of kitchenware dating from Victorian times right up to the 1960s. Downstairs were a number of tiny rooms, all filled to the brim with jewellery, dishes, glassware and clothes. It was an Aladdin's cave and she and Rachel had spent loads of time there. They had always come away with some small item; a jewellery box, a pretty tin, a lacy scarf, a ring, a bracelet, once even a pair of elbow-length gloves.

Rose stayed downstairs, smelling the dampish smell that she remembered from her last visit months and months before. She looked at the rows and rows of crystal wine glasses. She suddenly thought of Anna and wondered whether she would like this place. Probably not. Anna shopped in Harrods and Bond Street. This place would probably appal her. Joshua would like it, though. There was a room at the back chock-full of workmen's tools. She remembered the tiny bedroom he used in the house they'd lived in in Brewster Road. It was always crammed with bits of bikes and tools.

And then there was her mother. She would have loved this emporium. Her mother adored old things and scoured charity shops for old glasses or vases or crockery. She bought blouses and jackets from jumble sales and internet sites. Going to work her mother was one person; smart suit, shoes and briefcase. At weekends and holidays she wore this eclectic mix; a floral skirt, a tweed jacket, suede boots and round her neck a lace scarf that Brendan had bought her for a Christmas present. It was old, she'd said, the lace fragile; a stiff breeze might have blown a hole in it. Her mother was like two different people.

Now, though, Rose thought that her mother, Kathy Smith, was like three different people; policewoman, mother and . . . Who was the third person? The woman who had planned her own disappearance, who had left her daughter to live a lonely life?

Rose picked up a bead bangle from a shelf of glittering jewellery. Rachel had bought her one just like it, the beads turquoise and irregular like small polished stones. She'd given it to her after the summer holidays when Rose had fallen out with her. She'd got back to school a day before Rose. When Rose arrived she saw a small brown box on her pillow with the word *Sorry!* written on the front. Inside was the gift. Rose replaced the bangle on the shelf with the rest of the jewellery. Then she walked out of the emporium and along the street until she came to a tiny square that had benches in the middle. She sat down and watched people walking by.

The summer holidays after Rachel's lie had seen emails flying back and forth between them. Rachel was sorry. Rachel was sorry the whole summer long.

I was depressed; the summer was coming up; I didn't want to go home: I was worried about my mum's boyfriend, Robert, so I made the stupid story up; don't ask me why; I'm just an idiot.

Sometimes I think my life is just so dull that I have to make things up.

You've had dramatic things happen in your life. You don't know what it's like to be ordinary.

The only thing that ever happened to me was Juliet's death and that's not something I want to remember. Maybe that's why I made it up. Something to feel bad about that hadn't actually happened.

I promise I'll never lie about anything again.

Rose softened. Rachel had admitted she'd lied, she'd even tried to analyse it. Maybe this was a new beginning for her. In any case, the first days of the holidays when Rose was resolved to breaking up with her friend were grim. Walking around her grandmother's house it was as though she was the twelve-year-old who had first gone to live there. She had gone back three years in time, alone, friendless. All she had to look forward to was a solitary time at school. Rachel would find new friends and she, who did not easily connect with people, would be on her own.

It made her feel bereft.

When the emails came she ignored them for a few days but eventually she answered, stiffly and showing the hurt she'd felt at Rachel's lie. Then her answers got longer and she even tried to sympathise with Rachel, cheering her up, asking her about the terrible Robert and about how things were going with her dad's new wife, Melissa.

Rose wore the bracelet and she gave the silver locket she'd bought to Rachel. The friendship was strong again for the first few weeks of the autumn term. The cold weather stopped them going to the wood and they spent most of their time inside. There was work to do; exams were at the end of year and the school was geared up to getting high results for all their students. There were extra classes and regular tests. There were pastoral meetings and targets and work patterns were examined and commented on. The girls were put on notice.

This was the year of examinations and they had to knuckle down.

Rose did everything that was asked of her. She intended to get into university in three years' time. She wanted a career and life away from Anna and independence was the only way she was going to have that.

Rachel was less motivated and Rose saw it as her job to chivvy her along, to nag her about work, to make sure she was completing assignments. Rachel was easily bored, though, and didn't like the work. During private study time Rose saw her sitting in the refectory or in the quad chatting to other girls. Her grades were poor and Rose tried to explain to her how she needed to do more research or spend longer doing fresh drafts of her essays but Rachel told her, jokily, 'Give it a rest!' Or 'Leave me alone!'

They fell out bitterly just before half-term in October.

Rachel had said she would see her in the library after the last class. She was doing some research for a project on Buddhism and Rose said that she would help. Rose went to the library and waited for her. She took her book out and read for a while. She went on to one of the monitors and looked up websites she liked. Eventually, she gave up and went to look for Rachel. A girl she asked said she'd seen Rachel go into Brontë House. A feeling of indignation took hold of her. Rachel had no right to be in Brontë House when she'd agreed to meet Rose in the library. She marched across and found Rachel sitting in a small kitchen with two other girls, one of them Tania Miller. She walked right in and stood stiffly amid them. They were sitting on high stools at the breakfast bar. She gave Rachel a glare but all Rachel said was 'Oh, hi!' and kept talking. She stood uncertainly. Eventually she pulled a chair out from a table and sat on it feeling ignored. She was on a lower level than the three of them and as she looked up at Rachel's smiling face, her hands gesticulating, she felt a hot flicker of jealousy.

How easy Rachel was with other people.

Tania was listening to Rachel's story with the beginnings of a smile on her face. When Rachel finished Tania clapped her hands together with glee.

This was how Rachel spent her time instead of working, instead of being with Rose. She got up suddenly and walked out of the kitchen. She got as far as the door of Brontë House and stopped.

What was wrong with her?

Rachel was only talking to some other girls! She turned and walked back towards the tiny kitchen and heard a tinkle of laughter coming from the room. When she got closer she heard Rachel's voice loud and clear. 'God! Take no notice of Rose. She's so possessive and needy! It's driving me completely nuts.'

She walked into the kitchen and stared at her friend. Her eyes bored into Rachel's face. How could she say that? Without a single word she walked out again.

Moments later she heard Rachel following her along the path.

'Rose, don't be silly. I was only joking,' she called.

Rose kept her head down and walked rapidly. She reached her own room and locked the door from the inside and ignored Rachel knocking and calling out to her. The next day she got up early and packed her bag for the half-term break. Then she walked to the bus stop and went into Holt by herself. It wasn't allowed but she didn't care and she stayed there all day until she was sure that Rachel would have left for the half-term holidays.

The friendship should have ended then.

But after half-term Rachel came back to school unrepentant.

There had been no emails asking for forgiveness and when Rose saw her coming and going Rachel was cold and distant. She saw her a lot with Tania Miller and the girls from Brontë House. It was as if she was the one who had offended Rachel and not the other way round. Rose was being punished and instead of making her resolute and aloof it made her miserable and sad.

She wanted the friendship back.

She had gone over the top and been too possessive. Maybe the fact that she was alone in the world meant that she leant too much on her friend. She could change. She could be less *needy*.

She wrote a letter. She said she was sorry and that she'd

been too heavy-handed and interfered too much in Rachel's work. She wanted to be friends again and this time she would not be possessive. This time the friendship would be different. She put the envelope under Rachel's door late one evening and then she waited. Five minutes later the envelope appeared under her door. Delighted, she picked it up. Inside Rachel had scribbled the words, *I've missed you! Let's be friends again! See you at breakfast. Luv Rachel* She looked wistfully at the adjoining wall. Rachel was only metres away. Why hadn't she come and knocked on her door, invited her into her room? Why had she not been keen to catch up, to talk over what had happened, to give her a hug? She lay down on her bed. She could not go next door now. She would have to wait until the morning.

At breakfast Rachel was pleased to see her and friendly. Instead of waiting for her to finish her food, though, she got up and headed off to class saying, 'See you later.' And Rose had smiled and watched her go. Later that day she saw her with Tania Miller out by the boating lake. The two of them were walking round together. She stared at Rachel who was talking and laughing. Each movement, each shake of the head, each gesticulation sent a dull pain through Rose and she turned away. She wondered whether they really were friends again or whether Rachel was playing some kind of game.

* * *

The sound of a text startled Rose. It broke her reverie. She registered the brightness of the day and the fact that she was there in Holt. It was not a year ago when she was desperately trying to be friends with Rachel again. She felt the tension fall away as she read the text message. It was from Amanda. **Meet you in the Cosy Cafe in 5 mins.**

She made her way towards a cafe and delicatessen in the middle of the town. Amanda and Molly were already inside sitting down. Rose got a peppermint tea and sat with them. She blew the steam from the top of the glass and stirred it with a long spoon. Molly was elbowing Amanda and nodding over towards the deli counter where a young man in a white apron was serving customers.

'It's Tim Baker,' Amanda said, explaining. 'I wonder if he knows about Rachel?'

Rose looked over, interested.

''Course he does,' Molly said.

'He doesn't look too upset.'

'Juliet Baker's brother?' Rose said, vaguely remembering Rachel telling her about him.

Amanda nodded, her mouth full of cake.

'Why should he be upset about Rachel?'

'He went out with Rachel. He was her boyfriend,' Molly said.

'He wasn't really her *boyfriend* as such,' Amanda said.

'He was.'

'For a couple of weeks! Rachel saw him for a couple of weeks. That hardly translates as boyfriend/girlfriend.'

Rose was looking from Amanda to Molly and back again.

'It was more than a couple of weeks. In any case it was full on. He used to come up to the school in his BMW at night and she'd slip out of the laundry back door. She used to text me and I'd go down and open it for her when she got back,' Molly said.

'Going out of the building at night is an automatic suspension,' Amanda said.

'Rachel was in love.'

'No, she wasn't. It only lasted a couple of weeks.'

Amanda caught Rose's eye. She had a look of exasperation on her face. Molly was fiddling with the pink feather clip. Her hand came away holding one of the feathers. She placed the feather at the edge of the table.

'When did this happen?' Rose said.

'September. As soon as we got back,' Molly said, with a wary look at Amanda as if she expected her to interrupt. 'She knew him anyway from when she was friends with Juliet.'

'Was she upset when it finished?' Rose said, looking back at Molly.

'A lot. She *loved* him . . .'

'You don't fall in love with someone in two weeks,' Amanda said softly, as if she was talking to a young child.

'It was longer than two weeks,' Molly said sulkily.

Rose ate her cake. The two girls went silent. Amanda was looking at her phone but Molly was fiddling with the pink feather, brushing it back and forwards along the tablecloth.

They went for the bus soon after. Molly and Amanda were talking again but Rose lagged behind. She thought of the conversation they'd just had in the Cosy Café. Rachel had had a boyfriend. Not just any boyfriend but the brother of her old friend who had committed suicide. In the year that they'd been friends they'd talked about boys but that was all. They hadn't *known* any boys. Rachel had a couple of boy cousins that she sometimes referred to and there were the famous boys from Nelson Preparatory School some miles away and occasionally glimpsed in Holt.

How had they got together?

The bus was turning the corner heading towards their stop. Rose made a decision.

'You go on,' she said, laying her hand on Amanda's arm. 'I've just remembered something I needed to get. I'll get the next bus.'

She walked off in the direction of the Cosy Cafe.

THIRTEEN

Tim Baker was a good-looking boy.

Rose eyed him while pretending to look through packets of organic pasta. He was tall and had broad shoulders and muscular arms as if he played sport. His hair was cropped short but his sideburns were carefully shaped as though he took some interest in his appearance. He had a broad smile, showing straight white teeth, and an easy way with customers, chatting amiably with each one.

She had no idea whether he looked like his sister, Juliet. Rose had only seen pictures of her dotted around the school. She remembered the first time she ever heard the name was on the morning of the announcement of Juliet's death. It had been at a special assembly. At the end of morning classes the girls were called along to the main hall, all grumbling, aware of the precious minutes being cut off their lunch hour. Mrs Abbott was at the front, standing rigidly and looking deadly serious. After she informed the school, there were prayers and a moment's silence but Rose had had no idea what to think about. Juliet Baker was just a name for her. It didn't belong to anyone that she knew or could picture. Juliet was in Brontë House and even though some of those girls were in her classes she had never come face to face with the dead girl.

Mrs Abbott said nothing about the manner of Juliet's death. She said there had been a *terrible accident* and that we must *pray for Juliet and her family*. She did not say that Juliet Baker had hanged herself. That piece of information emerged in the next few days. It wasn't until months later, when she was friends with Rachel, that she heard the whole story.

How odd that Rachel should *go out* with Tim Baker.

The counter was clear now and Tim Baker was looking over in her direction, probably wondering why it was taking this girl so long to choose the type of pasta she wanted to buy. Rose walked across to the counter empty-handed.

'Excuse me, are you Tim Baker?'

He nodded, frowning.

'My name is Rose Smith. I used to be a student at Mary Linton School for Girls. I'm a friend . . . At least I was a friend of Rachel Bliss? I wonder would you have a few minutes to talk?'

'Why?' he said, looking at her with hostility.

'It's nothing bad. It's just that I hadn't seen her for

months and I wanted to talk to someone who'd seen her more recently? Just five or ten minutes?'

He stared at her in a disconcerting way so that she had to break eye contact. When she looked back he had softened.

'I've got a break in half an hour. I'll be in the King's Head.'

'OK. I'll see you then.'

The King's Head was busy and Rose managed to get a couple of seats on the end of a table. There was a roaring fire at the far side of the bar but where she was sitting it was quite draughty. She held the edges of her coat together. Looking down she saw her black DMs tightly laced up, a rim of pink showing from the sock underneath. She was glad she'd dressed warmly this morning. She sipped her drink grimacing at its coldness. Tim Baker arrived moments later and went straight to the bar without so much as a wave in her direction. After paying for his drink he headed for her table and sat down opposite her. Finally, after taking a gulp of his beer, he looked at her.

'What can I do for you?' he said, in a mock deli-counter voice.

There was noise from all around, a dozen conversations going at once. She raised her voice.

'Rachel and I were friends for a year or so but we . . . We drifted apart and I hadn't seen her for months. One of the girls in school said you and she went out together. I just wondered how she was. Whether you thought she was unhappy?'

'We got together for a few weeks, end of September, early October. I saw her around and we got talking about Juliet. Actually, I felt a bit sorry for her. She seemed quite lonely. I know that she was always *available*, if you know what I mean.'

Rose didn't answer.

'Two, three weeks. We spent a bit of time together. That was it.'

'Did you end it?'

'No one really ended it. I said I'd ring her and I didn't. You know, I did feel sorry for her and at first it was nice to have someone to talk to about Juliet but after a while it brought back too many memories. It wasn't going anywhere. Look, she was an attractive girl and she . . .'

'What?'

'She was easy-going, if you know what I mean.'

Rose frowned. Tim Baker was smirking.

'There was no romance. It was just having a good time. And she was willing.'

'It was just about sex?'

'Don't look so shocked. On second thoughts, I get why you're shocked. You don't look like the sort of girl who . . .'

He looked her up and down, his eyes lingering on her heavy boots.

'Are you not interested in boys?'

Rose was instantly angry.

'You don't know me,' she snapped, tucking her boots back under the seat.

Tim Baker shrugged and looked around the pub. He didn't seem so good-looking now. His skin was red and his nose a little crooked. Rose swallowed hard and forced herself to talk to him.

'I just wanted to ask you if you thought, during those weeks, that she seemed a bit depressed? Only she wrote to me a week ago asking for my help and the odd thing is that she kept mentioning your sister, Juliet . . .'

'She wasn't depressed when she was with me. She seemed very happy, believe you me.'

He was so cocky. She disliked him intensely.

'Aren't you even sad that she's dead?' Rose said miserably.

'Listen,' he said, pushing his beer away as if he had no intention of drinking another drop of it, 'when my sister killed herself . . .'

He stared at her unable to finish his sentence. His eyes were heavy and she sensed some real unhappiness behind the good looks and the confidence.

'What was she like? I never knew her when I was at Mary Linton.'

He pulled his wallet out of his pocket and flipped it open. There, in a plastic pouch, was a photograph of a smiling girl. Juliet Baker. This picture was different to the ones she had seen around the school. Those were formal shots, usually in school uniform. She picked up Tim Baker's wallet and looked closely at the image in front of her. A pale face surrounded by black jaw-length hair, the fringe brushed to the side. She was smiling widely, her teeth white and even just like her brother's. She was pretty and there was a spark of something joyful about her.

'When was this taken?'

'A few months before . . .'

'I'm sorry.'

'You didn't even know her!'

'No, but I know what it's like to lose someone.'

He shook his head and stood up.

'I'm done talking about Rachel,' he said. 'I know you said that she was your friend but she wasn't a nice person. I didn't have any feelings at all when I heard she'd died. I'm not sorry. Not one bit.'

She watched him walk out of the bar. The door opened and let in a blast of cold air and she nursed her drink for a few moments before getting up herself and leaving the pub.

On the bus she thought of what he'd said about Rachel. *She was easy-going*. Was that all it had been about? Was that why Rachel was so down? Because the boy she had slept with had dumped her without even a goodbye? Were the supposed sightings of Juliet Baker just one of Rachel's little fantasies when, actually, what she had was an ordinary, everyday broken heart?

She thought of Joshua. How different he was to Tim Baker. She could never imagine him talking about a girl like Tim Baker had. Joshua had lost his dad but had no bitterness in him. He wouldn't take it out on other people.

That's why she cared for Joshua so much.

She stared out of the window at the countryside speeding past. Why was she there, on the bus, spending time in her past life? Rachel was dead. She'd brought the letters. Why not just leave it at that? Why should she care what state of mind Rachel was in? Maybe she should pack up and head for Stiffkey and be with Joshua.

She walked from the bus stop back towards the school. She put her hands in her pockets, feeling the cold air nipping at her. A couple of cars passed and when she got to the entrance of the school she looked at the grass verge alongside it where Joshua had pulled up in Skeggsie's Mini to drop her off. It was rutted with tyre tracks for ten metres or so, as though a number of cars had pulled up here to drop people off or pick them up. Possibly Tim Baker's BMW had sat there some nights waiting for Rachel to creep out through the laundry room to get out of school.

She turned into the driveway and walked slowly, not really wanting to arrive back at the school again. She wondered how Joshua was getting on and pulled her phone out of her pocket to see if she had any messages. There were no missed calls or texts. Maybe she should contact him and tell him she wanted to go back to London. Anna's house seemed homely after being back in school. She wished she was back in her studio, listening to music, sketching or working on her laptop. Why not call him? If they left soon they could be back in London by teatime.

Then she took a deep breath. It would be unfair to do that. Joshua had come to explore the areas on his father's map. It was important to him. He had sounded excited in his emails. She would only drag him back before he'd found whatever it was he was looking for. In any case, she'd said she would speak to the police. In less than twenty-four hours' time she would be done with the school and on her way home.

She quickened her step.

Nearing the main building she saw groups of girls out of uniform walking or running across the grounds. It was Saturday afternoon. There was always a variety of sports activities, choir, music practice and drama clubs. As well as that, it was time to just run off and explore the grounds and find somewhere private to be away from the building and the kindly but prying eyes of the housemistresses. She got as far as the quad and stopped. It was 2.30. The police were due in school at three to speak to some of the staff and the girls. She was hot after the walk so she decided to sit for a while rather than go back up to her room.

She looked idly round at the groups of girls. A great guffaw of laughter erupted from a group of younger girls in jeans and brightly coloured sleeveless puffa jackets. She looked down at her own clothes. White sweatshirt, black trousers, grey coat. Tim Baker had thought her dull, uninteresting. *You don't look like the sort of girl who . . .* What did he mean? Not the sort of girl who likes boys? Who boys like? Not *easy-going*?

Did she care?

She would certainly never be interested in anyone like Tim Baker. Puffed-up and arrogant, he reminded her of some of the boys at her high school in London. They walked around looking at their own reflections in shop windows, constantly aware of their own ability to attract girls. Joshua wasn't like that. He seemed completely unselfconscious. Uninterested in how he looked or seemed to other people. He was attractive, she knew that. The girl, Clara, came into her head and she felt a moment's anguish. Clara who had visited the flat and gone along with Joshua when he went to the Russian cafe in South Kensington. Was she his girlfriend?

Don't think about it, Rose! she said to herself.

She looked up at the school building, her eyes inevitably drawn to the top floor and the window of her old room. Then she looked along at the room next door, Rachel's room. There was a face looking out.

It startled her. She sat upright and stared at it. It was a girl looking out at the grounds. She remembered Rachel's letter and how she had described seeing the face of Juliet Baker in her room. Rachel thought she had seen a ghost.

Who was it? Why was this person in Rachel's room?

She stood up and walked purposefully towards the entrance of the building.

This was no ghost but Rose wanted to know who it was.

FOURTEEN

'What are you doing in here?' Rose said.

The door to Rachel's room was open. A girl spun round and stared at her. She had short hair, tightly cut. She looked familiar and it took a few seconds for Rose to recognise her.

'Tania!' she said.

It was Tania Miller, the girl from Brontë House who Rachel had had an on-off friendship with.

'Sorry, I didn't recognise you . . .'

Tania looked so different. Her glossy hair had gone and now her face was rounder and her mouth seemed fuller. The hair that Rose had admired had dominated her face and now she just looked fresher, nicer somehow.

'I like the hair.'

Tania shrugged. 'When did you turn up?'

'Yesterday. I came because . . . Well, I heard about Rachel.'

The mention of Rachel's name made Tania flinch. Rose looked awkwardly around the room.

'I just came up for a look . . .' Tania said, answering the unasked question. 'I was just curious. Turns out it's just an empty room.'

Rose nodded. Tania seemed about to say something then shook her head.

'I'm sorry for her,' Rose said. 'You know we'd stopped being friends but I wouldn't have wanted anything to happen to her.'

Tania nodded. She seemed on the brink of tears.

'But you and she, you were friends in Brontë and afterwards.'

'On and off.'

'That's how it was with Rachel. On and off.'

Tania managed a smile but her lips looked strained.

'I'll see you round,' she said and walked past Rose and out of Rachel's room.

Rose went to follow her but then changed her mind. She stepped into Rachel's room and closed the door behind her. She sat on the end of the bed and looked around. There was nothing of Rachel's left in there. The bed was stripped and all the paraphernalia of a teenage girl had been packed away.

Who had done this, she wondered. One of the cleaning staff or maybe Martha Harewood? She pictured the house-mistress for a second, moving quietly around Rachel's

room, folding up clothes, covering pictures and ornaments with bubble wrap, tidying up toiletries into a box
or bag. Books would have gone in one of the sturdy card-
board boxes that the girls were given at the end of every
summer term. Everything had to be cleared to allow the
room to be cleaned thoroughly for the new term.

Where were Rachel's things? In the basement?
Locked away in some cupboard? Rose sighed. How
different the room was without the posters and books
and ornaments that Rachel had. It looked naked, empty;
as if it had been robbed.

Rose had loved to spend time in Rachel's room. In the
early days they had spent a part of every evening in there.
It was a place to read bits of books out loud, to listen to
music, to use the laptops side by side.

Often they would talk about important things. This
was where Rose first told Rachel about her mother's job,
how she and Brendan Johnson met while working in the
same police sector. How they followed up cold cases to
see if they could find clues that would catch the crimi-
nals. She told her that this was most probably the reason
that they were killed. She showed Rachel the photos she
had of her mother and Rachel gasped. 'She's really young-
looking! She's so pretty!'

Rachel described her father's new house and told her
how Melissa had fitted out a room for her to stay in

whenever she visited. *Melissa's a pain but she likes me! What can I do? I don't tell my mum about it.* She also talked about her mum's boyfriend, Robert. *He put his hand on my leg under the dinner table. My mum was next to me, talking. I got up and said I didn't feel like eating my dinner!* Rose was appalled. *You have to tell someone!* But Rachel shook her head. *I can't hurt my mum's feelings. I have to put up with it.*

When they'd exhausted all subjects they'd lie on the single bed, Rose up one end, Rachel at the other, and listen to music.

Then there were the Nails.

Rachel had an array of varnishes and equipment for manicure and pedicure. She did Rose's nails on a Friday night as nail varnish and some make-up was allowed over the weekend. She would make Rose sit in front of her with her hands resting on a pillow. She would lift each hand and massage it and shape each nail before painting it violet or turquoise or even black. During the week it was the toenails, easy to hide under socks and shoes. Rose loved the ritual. She felt the warmth of her friend's hands massaging her skin or pulling at her fingers, using cuticle creams and nail files. They gossiped and it seemed different sitting face to face instead of slouching around the school or whispering in corners. As if they were all grown-up, not schoolgirls at all.

Rose liked it when Rachel fussed over her.

But after the half-term argument things changed. Time in Rachel's room was limited and it only ever happened if Rachel wanted it. After Rachel replied to her letter and said they would be friends again, Rose had to wait for an invitation to go into her room. Sometimes it came and sometimes it didn't. Rose would lie on her bed late at night and wonder what Rachel was doing. Once or twice she heard low voices and went across to the wall to listen. She was sure that Rachel had Tania Miller in there even though it was against the rules for people from other Houses to visit after nine. There were whispers and giggles and Rose felt her throat dry as paper as she imagined Rachel and Tania in there; maybe Tania sitting facing Rachel while Rachel picked up her hand and did each nail carefully, rubbing lotion around the cuticles.

Then, one day, it all changed.

Rose went down to the refectory and saw Rachel on her own. She carried her tray over and sat down beside her, surprised to see her looking upset.

'What's up?' she said. 'Where's Tania?'

'We're not friends any more.'

'Oh.'

Rachel shrugged. 'She's a silly cow. I don't know why I bothered with her.'

Rose didn't know what to say. Inside she felt a spurt of delight. She wanted to smile, to go and sit next to Rachel and put her arm around her shoulder, to comfort and be the best of friends again but she sensed that this was the wrong thing to do so she finished her food slowly.

'Cheer up. I'll catch you later,' she said, taking her tray and heading away.

Leaving the refectory she couldn't stop herself smiling. That night, just after eight, she got a text from Rachel. **Come next door and listen to my new CD**. Rose waited five whole minutes before sending a reply. **Just finishing some work. See in you half an hour???** Thirty long minutes later she got up and went next door. Rachel was sitting cross-legged on the floor and patted the cushion next to her.

They were friends again.

Rose went to see the policewoman.

She introduced herself as WPC Lauren Clarke. The interview was in a conference room which was linked to Mrs Abbott's office. The head teacher left them alone and there was a few moments' quiet. The letters from Rachel were on the table between them. Each of them was in a plastic envelope. The WPC was reading over the letters.

'So, you were close friends with Rachel Bliss?'

'Well,' Rose said, blowing through her teeth, 'for about a year and then we weren't. That's why I did nothing when I got these letters.'

'You didn't see them as a cry for help?'

'Not at first. At first I was annoyed by them but when

they kept coming I asked my grandmother to ring the school. Particularly after Rachel phoned me and left messages. I knew there was something up with her. I mean she was always a bit dramatic but this . . .'

Rose gestured to the letters. The policewoman gave her a smile and then glanced across to a BlackBerry that was on the table beside her. She read something there, then turned back to Rose.

'These references to Juliet Baker. What did you make of that?'

Rose shrugged. She was beginning to feel uncomfortable. She had brought the letters to the school as evidence of something but she, herself, hadn't spoken to or set eyes on Rachel for five months. What was the point of asking her anything?

'I didn't really think anything of it. Rachel has – or had – a wild imagination. I just assumed it was something she was saying to . . .'

'You mean she was making it up?'

'Possibly. She did make things up when I was her friend.'

The policewoman nodded. She picked up her BlackBerry and frowned at it. Rose had the feeling that she was about to leave.

'Can I ask you how she died? Was it an accident?'

'It will be up to the inquest to determine that . . .'

'The girls are saying that there was alcohol. Was there anyone else involved?'

'I'm afraid I can't say. It's confidential. The inquest will . . .'

'I've come all the way from London to bring those letters,' Rose said. 'And I know you can't tell me anything for certain. I know you're not allowed to. My mother was a police officer so I know how it works but can't you tell me just off the record? I'm not going to say anything to anyone. I'm going back home tomorrow.'

'Your mother was a police officer?'

'Yes. She worked in Cold Cases.'

'Where? Round here? Might I have met her?'

'She disappeared five years ago,' Rose said, shaking her head. 'The police have told me that she is most probably dead.'

'Oh, that's awful. I don't know what to say. That's dreadful.'

'It was five years ago.'

'Still.'

'I know you can't give out information but I'm not a student here.'

'We are meant to keep information out of the public domain.'

'Off the record.'

'Well . . .'

'I won't tell anyone.'

She seemed to think about it for a minute.

'Preliminary reports suggest that she had been dead for

about six to seven hours when she was found. We'll know more after the autopsy this evening. There were suggestions of alcohol at the scene. It could have been an accident. A teenage girl who drinks too much and falls into the water. We get cases like this from time to time but they're usually in the summer months.'

'Rachel didn't drink when I knew her. She smoked but . . .'

'We know that she recently broke up with a boyfriend. Tim Baker. Maybe she was pining. I have yet to speak to him. Possibly he will throw some light on it.'

Rose frowned. She couldn't see Tim Baker being any help at all.

'She was friendly with a girl called Molly Wallace.'

'I've spoken to Molly. She's very upset. She says that Rachel told her to go away that evening. She wanted to be on her own.'

'But why go out to the lake? In such cold weather. You don't think she went out there with the intention of . . .'

'What?'

'Killing herself?'

Rose said the words out loud. She'd been trying not to think them ever since she'd heard that Rachel was dead. She looked at the policewoman optimistically, hoping she would say, *Oh no. It was definitely an accident.*

'It's a possibility that we are considering.'

'Did she leave a note?'

'No, but not everyone leaves a note. Her friend Juliet Baker didn't. It may be that the manner of *her* death affected Rachel deeply.'

'That was a long time ago.'

'Your letters mention the sightings of the dead girl, the boyfriend's sister. This girl was certainly in Rachel's mind constantly.'

'So, it's not really clear whether it was suicide or an accident?'

The policewoman sighed and touched the 'L' that was hanging on her chain.

'Like I say, we have to wait and see what the autopsy report brings. Your letters, of course, show her state of mind and some of the other girls have given statements which suggest she was acting erratically over the last weeks.'

'Right.'

'I know you said you weren't that friendly with her any more but it's still a bit of a blow, right? And on top of your mother disappearing. Look, here's my card. My mobile number and my email address are there. Contact me if you remember anything. I've got the BlackBerry. I pick up messages all the time.'

'I'll be going home tomorrow.'

'OK. We'll contact you if we need to. And, once again, very sorry about your mother. I don't just say this out of politeness. The police force hate to lose one of their own.

It's the worst thing.'

'Thank you.'

As Rose left the room Mrs Abbott called to her.

'Rose,' she said, 'would you mind terribly coming to meet Mr and Mrs Bliss tomorrow at twelve? They're coming to pick up Rachel's things and have said that they would like to meet some of her friends.'

Rose frowned. She did not want to meet anyone from Rachel's family.

'I'm due to go back to London,' she said.

'It would only be for ten, fifteen minutes. I thought that it would be nice for them to meet you. A friend who was with Rachel in happier times.'

She didn't answer.

'Rose, Miss Harewood told me that you had fallen out with Rachel but, now that she's gone, those kind of petty disagreements shouldn't matter. Just fifteen minutes. My office at twelve. I'll leave you to make up your own mind whether or not you come. You're a Mary Linton girl. I know you'll do the right thing.'

Rose walked away, feeling the head teacher's eyes on her back.

Back in her room she went to her laptop and found a message from Joshua.

Rose! You'll hardly believe this but I've found the place I was looking for. And it's marked on Dad's map. It's a cottage and it's on the edge of the mudflats a couple of kilometres outside Stiffkey. The coastal path that I told you about! It goes along the edge of fields and bracken and all you can see is the sky for miles around. There's a creek to cross and just along from that there's a path that goes off to the left. I went down it and found this deserted cottage. Its windows are covered with wood and the doors are padlocked. There's an outbuilding with a boat. The place is covered in cobwebs and looks as though no one has been anywhere near it for years.

I want you to come and see it with me. Tomorrow morning. Wear sensible shoes. It won't take long but you have to see it so that you don't think I'm mad. I could pick you up from the school gates at eight. It would take thirty minutes to get here and then I could drive you straight back to school so that you can finish up whatever it is that you're doing there.

Tonight, I'm seeing this local guy, Colin Crabtree, who knows a lot about Stiffkey and the houses around. He's a historian and he collects data about the village and its surroundings. The parish committee rooms have old maps and details of past tenants and he's going to show me those later tomorrow morning. After that I could come and pick you up and we could go back to London.

Does this sound OK! Does it give you enough time to finish stuff at the school! Josh XXXX

Rose sat back. Actually, she had finished what she had come to do at the school now. She would like to call a cab and go to Stiffkey and stay with Joshua until he had finished what he was doing. But he sounded busy and she would probably just drag him down. And she felt pressure to go and see Rachel's parents at twelve.

She typed out a reply.

Josh, see you in the morning at eight. Rose XXXX

FIFTEEN

Rose did not have a good night. Tossing and turning in her old bed, she woke up at 0.48, 2.37 and 5.44. At ten to six she got up and went to the toilet. When she came back she looked at the wrinkled bedding and decided that there was no point trying to sleep any more. She got her laptop out and went on her blog Morpho. She read over the stuff she'd written recently and then typed today's date and time and started to write.

Did Rachel commit suicide? That's what I'm wondering. Did she go out to the lake late in the evening, sure that no one would be around, drink herself stupid and slide into the water? Was this her way of ending her own life?
If I had rung her, listened to her story of woe, might things have been different? Or did she just go out to the lake because that's where she thought she saw the ghost of Juliet Baker. She was depressed and

> took the alcohol with her. When there was no ghost
> did she just sit herself down and get drunk? And,
> getting up to go back to school, did she lose her
> balance and topple into the water?
> If I had rung her, might I have been able to lighten
> her mood, make her feel better?

After she finished she shut down and felt disgruntled. Unloading her problems on to this dispassionate machine usually made her feel a bit better. Not this time.

She tiptoed along to the kitchen, made a cup of tea and took it back to her room. Instead of getting back into bed, she pulled the desk chair over to the window and drank it while she looked out at the grounds. The moon was fuzzy but gave enough light for her to see the lake and the boat-house. After a few moments, her eyes moved back towards the trees that edged the car park. She looked carefully along them. This was where Rachel had seen a *ghost*.

Rose shivered. The room was cold, the central heating hadn't yet come on. She finished her drink and got dressed quickly and then decided to pack. By the time she'd finished it was twenty to seven. Not too early to go and cook some breakfast. Then it would be time to walk up the drive and meet Joshua.

Skeggsie's Mini was parked in the same place when she arrived at the school gate. She was warm from the walk and went quickly across the lane and got into the car.

'Hi!' she said.

Joshua gave her a smile and started the car engine. She was so pleased to see him. It was as much as she could do not to put her hand out and ruffle his hair with sheer pleasure.

'You OK?' he said.

She nodded. He looked up to his rear-view mirror just as a car came speeding up the lane behind them, overtook the Mini and swung in front of them, parking on the verge a few metres ahead. Its brakes made a loud noise which jarred amid the early Sunday morning quiet of the country lane. It was a blue BMW.

'I wonder who that is?' Rose said.

Joshua pulled out into the lane and slowly passed the parked car. Rose looked round. The driver of the car was Tim Baker. At that moment someone emerged from the school drive. She recognised Tania Miller immediately even though her short hair was covered with a woolly hat. Tania skipped across the lane and got into the BMW.

Well, fancy that, Rose said to herself. *Tania Miller and Tim Baker.*

The journey was shorter than she had expected. They drove into the small village of Stiffkey, past the White Rose where Joshua was staying. A few moments later there was a turning on the right with a sign that read, *Beach*.

'There's a beach?'

'No. At least, there *is* one but it's twenty minutes' walk across the mudflats. If you know the paths, it's all right. Otherwise it's ankle-deep in sea water.'

Rose wrinkled her nose and looked down at her DMs. *Wear sensible shoes*, Joshua's email had read. That was all Rose had, sensible flat shoes or boots. Had he not noticed? She wondered how far they were going to have to walk to this place. The car moved slowly up the lane, the houses becoming fewer and more spaced out. To the right was a campsite, full of tents, caravans and mobile homes. In front of her Rose could see the horizon, stretching from side to side as if someone had drawn a line across the sky; the mudflats an expanse of flat grassland, reeds and bushes.

'What happened to the sea?'

'It's out there. You can smell it. You can feel it in the air but you can't see it.'

'Um.'

'I'm surprised you don't know. Didn't you go to school round here for years?'

They parked the car on a small area of tarmac.

'We never came anywhere like this.'

They got out. The slamming of the car doors sounded loud.

'Have we got to walk out there?' Rose said, pointing in the direction of the sea.

'No, the coastal path runs along here. It's dry, a bit muddy in places. It's about fifteen minutes' walk.'

They walked in silence for a while, Joshua in front, Rose a few paces behind. The track was wide enough for a vehicle and had tyre marks on either side, making muddy ruts which she tried to avoid stepping in. Some of the tracks veered off and seemed to head for the mudflats. Joshua turned and saw her looking at them.

'There are beaches out there, places where the sea comes in and areas of sand and rocks where people bathe. You have to know the tracks, though. That's what Colin Crabtree told me.'

Rose looked out at the mudflats, dirty greens merging into browns seeping away as far as the eye could see. She couldn't see any inlets and blue water although she could *feel* the presence of the sea, a tang of salt or brine in the air. In the sky the sun was hazy and high. It was cold, a bothersome breeze at the back of her neck.

'Colin Crabtree was a mine of information,' Joshua said, waiting for her to catch up and walk along beside him. 'He said that this place – he called it Fisherman's Cottage – has been empty for thirty years or more but people in the town thought that someone had bought it about fifteen years ago and began to renovate it, but then the work stopped and it was locked up again. He said that people who live in nearby houses say that they sometimes see a Land Rover driving down the lane towards it but then they don't see anything for months.'

'How do you know this is the right place?'

'I just know it is,' he said mysteriously, linking her arm and pulling her on, as if she was deliberately holding herself back.

The path came to a fork. Beyond it she could see some water in the distance, an inlet.

'That's the creek but we go down here.'

The track continued but the hedges were thicker and more spiky. Rose had to manoeuvre herself carefully, ducking from time to time to avoid being lacerated by thorny branches. Then, all of a sudden, they were out in the open and in front of them was a small slate-fronted cottage with boards nailed over the windows and a heavy front door. To the side of it was an outbuilding and in front was a garden which had been left untended. It looked as though it had been abandoned.

'This wasn't how you described it to me,' Rose said. 'You said it was white.'

'I know. I think I only had a *feeling* of this place. I knew it was a house and I supplied a picture of a house. I had an essence of it rather than a real image.'

Rose pursed her lips. She didn't want to fall out with Joshua but, really, hadn't he just found what he wanted to find? A map with a village marked on it. A derelict cottage. A feeling he had from an item of his dad's clothing? Did it mean any more than that?

'Come and look at the boat,' he said, walking towards the outbuilding.

He was excited, his face split with a smile. She followed him reluctantly.

'This door had a padlock but it just came apart when I fiddled with it, like it was only there for show.'

He pushed the door open and they walked into a big dark space. It had a musty damp smell. Up against the back wall was a boat. It was covered in tarpaulin and sat up high on wooden struts. Rose could see its hull curving down underneath the rubber covering and for a second she was reminded of the violin she owned that sat in her drawer at Anna's house, unused for months.

Joshua was at the door. 'Look at the house.'

He walked up to the front of the cottage. The door was solid wood and had two padlocks, one at the top and one three-quarters of the way down.

'One of these is newer than the other,' he said.

He cupped the lower padlock in his hand. It was brassy and looked as if it had been recently attached. Rose looked away, behind the plot. She could see fields and a copse. The sound of a car could be heard in the distance but she couldn't see any movement. It was a private place not overlooked by any other buildings. But so what?

'How can you be sure this has anything to do with

Brendan? There are probably dozens of buildings like this all along this coastline.'

'I knew you wouldn't believe me.'

'Aren't you just grasping at straws?'

He shook his head.

'I just know. This place was marked on Dad's map. It *feels* like the right place. In any case . . .'

She sighed and turned away. The breeze pulled her hair this way and that. What was she doing here? In the middle of nowhere? It was like no coastline she had ever visited and as far as she could tell she had never been anywhere like this with her mother or with Brendan and Joshua when they had lived together.

'I knew you would be like this,' Joshua said. 'I wouldn't have brought you here unless I was sure. Look.'

He took something out of his jacket pocket. It was the key ring he had got from the file of his dad's belongings. He held it out to her. It hung in the air between them.

'What?'

'Take it,' he said.

She took it from him, looking puzzled.

'Open the top padlock.'

She looked round at the door.

'It opens the lock? You've already done it?'

'Just open it, Rosie. Just to satisfy yourself,' he said, more sternly.

She walked to the door and reached up to the silver padlock, tarnished and grimy-looking. The key in contrast was bright and shiny. She slid it into the lock and tried to turn it. It wouldn't budge so she went on tiptoes and tried again and it turned, the padlock opening like the claw of a crab.

'Oh.'

'This is it, Rosie. This place is something to do with Dad and Kathy and what happened to them. If I had a crowbar I could get the other padlock off and look inside.'

'Break in?'

'Not today, no. But I'm seeing Colin Crabtree again this morning so I should be able to get some more information on it. I'm also going to contact our solicitors. If this place is Dad's, then it should belong to me now. Then I can get into it legally.'

If this place is Dad's. Whenever Joshua got excited about finding something out he always assigned it to Brendan. He seemed to forget that her *mother* went missing as well.

'We should get back,' she said, shivering.

'Can't you at least pretend to be interested?'

'In what? Some derelict building? Maybe it is your dad's. Maybe he did own it but *look*, no one's been here for years. It doesn't tell us anything!'

Joshua blew through his teeth and walked off back in the direction of the coastal path. He was annoyed with her. What had he expected? She followed him and thought back some weeks to when they'd first found out startling things about their parents' disappearance. She had been sceptical but he had drawn her into it and she had hoped that something would emerge from their search.

Then he had been right to push her.

'Josh,' she called after him but he didn't turn round.

She hurried after him.

She was sceptical. The cottage felt like nothing to do with anything. This seemed like something of Joshua and Brendan's. Possibly some holiday home that Brendan had bought and tried to renovate for a while. Maybe it was when Joshua was a baby or toddler and he had some deep memories of it. So what if the key was in Brendan's stuff next to a place marked on a map. Wouldn't Brendan necessarily have a key to it if it was his holiday home?

But geographically this place didn't feel important at all. Her mother and Brendan went missing after having a meal in a restaurant in Islington, in the heart of London. Rose and Joshua now knew that they had taken a plane to Warsaw. After that there was no further information.

Except for the notebooks and the picture of Viktor Baranski, the Russian man who had been found dead off the North Norfolk coast. But Rose had no idea if the notebooks had anything to do with her mother and Brendan or if they were just some weird possession of Frank Richards, the man who had told them that their parents were alive.

Frank Richards. She'd thought about him just the previous evening. She pictured him weeks before as he'd walked out of his flat, pulling a suitcase on wheels behind him. He'd put his arm out to hail a taxi, then gave her the phone number. It was his job, Frank Richards told her, to look after her while her mother was out of her life.

Was it true? Or just some fantasy of a deranged man? He had certainly shown, by other things that he had done, that he was dangerous and unpredictable. But Rose had kept the phone number, anyway. She'd tapped it into her mobile with the name Frank Richards as if he was just like any other contact she had. Now and then she'd taken her phone out and accessed the number and just stared at it. The numerals sat solidly on the tiny screen and yet to her the letters were indistinct and fragile.

'Come on, Rose.'

Joshua was calling her *Rose*. This almost always meant that he was upset. The car was up ahead and she was glad to get in out of the chilly breeze.

'I'm sorry,' she said when they were sitting in the car. 'I should have been more positive. I just don't seem to be able to take this seriously.'

'Because of what I told you about my dad's jumper? The idea of anything *supernatural*?'

She shrugged. She thought of Juliet Baker supposedly appearing in the school almost two years after she committed suicide.

'Not everything can be explained by science,' he said.

'That's the last thing I ever thought I'd hear you say.'

'Years ago people said that schizophrenics were possessed by the devil. Now they understand the disease and know that people really *hear* voices. There's nothing supernatural about it.'

'So?'

'So maybe that feeling I had isn't anything to do with ghosts, maybe it's some sort of psychic energy. We don't understand it now but in years to come . . .'

Rose couldn't stop shaking her head.

'Right,' Joshua said in a clipped voice, starting the car, doing a rapid reverse up the tiny car park. 'I shouldn't have said anything.'

He drove out of the car park and down the lane. Once on the road he speeded up and they sat in silence the whole way back to the school. When they arrived at the gate she noticed, with surprise, that it was almost 10.30.

'I've got to get my stuff from the pub, see Colin Crabtree and then I'll come and pick you up. Shall I say one o'clock? Here or up at the school?' he said in a flat voice.

'At the school,' she said.

She got out of the car. He drove off without waving. She huffed. She was cross with herself. Why couldn't she have pretended she believed it? What difference would it have made? Crossing the road to the school entrance she was reminded of Tania Miller getting into Tim Baker's BMW. She wondered if it was significant or just another random fact that had nothing to do with anything else.

SIXTEEN

Back at Mary Linton there was over an hour to go until she was due to meet Rachel's parents. She decided to get a coffee and a sandwich from the refectory. She saw Molly sitting on her own and after she'd paid she walked across and sat down opposite her.

'Hi,' she said.

'Hello, Rose.'

'How are you feeling?'

'All right.'

'Where's Amanda?'

'Not sure.'

There was an uneasy silence. Rose spoke.

'So you and Rachel became friends,' she said softly, undoing the cellophane on her sandwich.

'Yes.'

'How did that happen? I mean, how did you hook up together?'

'We were in some of the same classes. She was kind of

fed up with the kids in the common room and so we spent a lot of time in her room.'

Rose didn't comment. It sounded like Rachel.

'I know Amanda didn't rate Rachel and I know you fell out with her but I liked her.'

'Did you know that Rachel thought she'd seen a ghost?' Molly nodded.

'She wrote and told me about it. She was quite upset . . .'

'Wrote to you?'

'Three letters. I brought them with me and gave them to the police.'

'She didn't say.'

'She was obviously going through a bad time. It was good that she had you here.'

Molly seemed ill at ease. She was fiddling with a slide in her hair, taking it off, putting it back on again.

'Rachel made me swear not to tell anyone about the ghost. She was afraid people would think she had gone mad. She saw it once in her room and then at night down by the car park. She said it looked like Juliet Baker.'

'Was she was just making it up?'

'No. It really seemed as though she *believed* it.'

'But with Rachel it was often difficult to tell when she was telling the truth. She was a strange girl.'

Molly looked thoughtful.

'She did get depressed. When it started, this ghost stuff, I asked her if she thought that it might have something to do with guilt feelings about Juliet Baker's death. You know how they say that when people commit suicide their family and friends suffer with guilt. Because they think they should have done something? Then she got *really* upset. *What have I got to feel guilty about?* she said. *I've got nothing to feel guilty about. Juliet Baker killed herself because of her father. Nothing to do with me!'*

'Her father?'

'He was a gardener here, in the school. He lost his job. He wasn't here long and then he was made redundant.'

'That's right. He was a gardener. I remember Rachel telling me when I first knew her,' Rose said, trying to picture the various men who had pottered around the gardens over the years.

'Anyhow, getting made redundant upset him badly, that's what Rachel told me.'

'What's that got to do with Juliet's suicide?'

'It wasn't long after that she died.'

Rose bit her lip. The second half of her sandwich sat uneaten.

'Here's Amanda,' Molly said.

Molly waved and Rose looked over to the swing doors and saw Amanda walking into the refectory. She came straight across to them. She had her laptop under her arm and some books in her hand. She got to the table and laid them all down. She looked fed up.

'Finished the essay?' Molly asked.

'First draft. Hi, Rose!'

She began to pat her pockets and tutted.

'What's up?' Molly said.

'I must have left my phone in the library!'

'I'll get it,' Molly said, getting straight up. 'You sit there. You look tired out. Where were you sitting?'

'In the carrel by the stained-glass window.'

'Back in a mo!'

Rose watched Molly walk off across the refectory, side-stepping tables and darting out of the door. She wanted to roll her eyes at Amanda, but Amanda was looking after Molly with concern.

'One minute she's OK, the next she's in floods of tears. I think she should go home for a break.'

'She seems genuinely upset about it.'

'She liked Rachel. One of the few who did. I think Rachel just used her. She needed someone to let her back into the building when she was bunking off with Tim Baker.'

'When they went out in the BMW?'

'Not just that,' Amanda said, looking round and lowering her voice. 'Molly told me they used to go into the boathouse. His father had a key from when he worked in the school. Tim used it whenever he wanted to . . .'

'The boathouse?' she said, picturing Tim Baker with his smart clothes and good looks through the dusty windows of the boathouse. The only thing she had ever seen in there were boats and spiders' webs.

'There's a tiny room at the back.'

Rose would have been surprised or shocked had she not already spoken to Tim Baker. Amanda looked stern.

'Molly was shocked when Rachel told her what they got up to. I think she probably exaggerated to show how grown-up she thought she was.'

'I spoke to Tim Baker yesterday. He didn't have a good thing to say about Rachel. Then I saw him this morning, waiting in his BMW outside the school gates and the next minute Tania Miller came out and got in beside him!'

'I knew that. I saw Tania with him in Holt last Saturday.'

'Rachel can't hold on to people. They get to know what she's really like . . .'

'You liked her once,' interrupted Amanda. 'There must have been something about her . . .'

'Yes, at first. On the surface. But underneath she was a mess.'

'Molly probably saw it as a challenge. She likes helping people. And with Rachel being on her own . . .'

'Like me. I was on my own, then Rachel came along.'

'People tried to make friends with you, Rose, but you were too offish. You always walked around school as though you didn't need anyone. Then, once you had Rachel, you hardly spoke to anyone else. You and she spent far too much time together.'

Rose bristled. It was the second time in two days that Amanda had ticked her off.

'Sorry, I'm just being truthful.'

Molly was coming back across the refectory.

'Here you are!' she said breathlessly, giving Amanda her phone.

Molly sat down. She had cheered up and was talking to Amanda about some girls they knew and Rose looked at the rest of her sandwich and decided she didn't want it. She said goodbye and headed upstairs to Eliot House and back to her old room.

Once inside she sat on the bed. She was feeling chastened by the conversation. And she had to admit that Amanda was right. In those last months she and Rachel had spent far too much time together.

After Rachel fell out with Tania, Rose and Rachel became much closer. Rose remembered the weeks when Rachel had cold-shouldered her. She hadn't wanted it to be like that again. She treasured the affection that Rachel gave her and after their horrible falling-out she was determined to make things different.

When she returned to school after the Christmas holidays she virtually picked Rachel up and spun her round, she was so pleased to see her.

But it didn't last. The old problems surfaced.

Schoolwork was hard; weekly tests and extra revision

assignments. Rose did it all, her room becoming a kind of huge filing cabinet for the twelve different subjects she was taking. Rachel fell behind, her room looking wrecked, with paper everywhere and books strewn about. Rose didn't comment or nag. This time she was going to leave Rachel to do what she wanted.

In February Rachel had to go home for a week because her mother was ill. When she came back she was depressed and moody. A couple of times, after Rose had finished revising for the evening, she knocked on Rachel's door and there was no answer. She lay awake till gone eleven and heard Rachel coming back, opening her door quietly. No doubt she'd been in some cubbyhole lighting up, a window open nearby to let the smoke out.

Rose didn't pry but she did ask her about the trip home.

'Mum and Robert are going to get married,' Rachel said miserably. 'I can't believe I'm going to have him living in the house all the time!'

'Why don't you tell someone about it?'

'I can't. It would upset Mum! Anyway, I don't really want to talk about it. Why don't I do your nails?'

'Go on then,' Rose said. 'Do the light pearl colour. No one will notice it.'

Rachel took her time, filing each nail carefully. They sat on the floor face to face, Rose's back to the bed. Rachel was outwardly concentrating on the nails but Rose felt sure her friend was thinking of something else. She could almost *feel* the weight on Rachel's shoulders.

'Did something happen?' Rose said. 'Last week, when you were at home?'

Rachel was looking down at her nails. She shook her head firmly but did not speak. Rose pulled her hand away and forced Rachel to look at her.

'Something happened, didn't it? What happened?'

Rachel's eyes were glistening with tears. She turned away from Rose and grabbed the box of tissues and blew her nose.

'What happened, Rachel?'

'Robert came into my room.'

Rose tensed.

'I can't keep my door locked all the time. I just can't. My mum will work out that something's wrong! Anyway, my mum had already gone to bed and I left Robert watching a movie on the telly and I got into bed and turned the light off and I must have dozed off because I felt this weight on one side of my bed. I opened my eyes and he was sitting there. It was dark. The whole house was dark and he was sitting there looking at me.'

'Oh.'

'I said, *What are you doing*! Like in a loud whisper and he was just staring at me.'

Rose felt her neck tighten.

'He put his hand out and touched my face and he said,

You're so beautiful. That's what he said. *You're so beautiful!'*

'What did you do?'

'I pulled away, I sat up. I put my light on and I pulled the duvet up to my neck. Then he got up and walked away, back to my mum's room. The next morning when my mum was in the kitchen and I was in the living room he came in and put his mouth right up to my ear and he whispered, *I won't forget last night*. And then he went to work.'

Rose put her hand out and grabbed Rachel's arm. Her skin felt clammy.

'It's creeping me out. I locked my door after that but if him and Mum get married I don't know what I'm going to do!'

'Can't you talk to your dad about it?'

'I can but what will happen? My dad'll go and knock him out and then my mum will know. I just don't know what to do!'

Rachel wasn't crying but she looked lost. Rose swivelled round and sat beside her and hugged her. She felt a rush of affection for this troubled girl. She had her own problems but Rachel's seemed more urgent. If something wasn't done she would have to live under the same roof as this man.

'Can't you write your mum a letter or something? Your mum would be horrified if she knew what was going on.

You don't want her to marry a creep like that, do you? You'd be doing her a huge favour.'

'You're right. You're right. I will. I'll write to her. I'll do it tomorrow. I'll show you the letter.'

Rose smiled. Maybe there really was an easy way out of this situation for her friend. The next day she waited to see the letter but it didn't come. *What about the letter?* Rose said. *I'm doing it tonight,* Rachel said but still it didn't come. A week later Rose found Rachel in tears, in the refectory. She'd just had a ticking off for not keeping her History work up to date and she was looking rough, her hair unwashed and pulled back into a tie. Her eyelids looked slightly swollen as if she'd been crying.

'What's the matter?' Rose said, fearful. 'Is it something to do with Robert?'

'He's taking Mum and me to Paris at Easter. Just the three of us. I don't want to go but how can I say no?'

'You need to tell someone about this!' Rose said, a hint of anger in her voice.

'I spoke to him on the phone. Mum said, *Speak to Rachel, tell her about the trip!* He came on the phone and it sounded as though Mum had gone off somewhere because he said, *I've bought you some pretty underwear.*'

Rose stared at her. Rachel was looking forlorn, hopeless. Someone had to put a stop to it. This man could not wheedle his way into Rachel's life. Someone had to inform the authorities. Rachel was too scared to do it.

It was up to Rose. She had to do something.

Now Rose packed her stuff. After she finished she pulled the bedding off the bed and dumped it in the corner.

She left her room and paused at Rachel's door. It was unlocked so she pushed it open. She stepped inside and went over to the window. She looked at the boathouse. She thought of what Amanda had said and pictured Tim Baker and Rachel sneaking into the building late at night. Tim Baker with his cocksure attitude. When she'd known Rachel neither of them had even *kissed* a boy. How she had changed in a few short months? Or was it, as Molly had said, that she had fallen *in love*?

Maybe that was the answer. Rachel had given herself to Tim Baker and then he dropped her. All the stuff about Juliet Baker's ghost was just another one of her stories.

She had a broken heart. She drank a lot of alcohol and fell in the lake.

An accident.

Not Rose's responsibility. She so wanted to believe that.

She left the room and went downstairs to the reception area, put her rucksack in the corner and reluctantly went to Mrs Abbott's room to meet Rachel's parents.

SEVENTEEN

Rose sat in the corrridor. She could hear voices from the head teacher's room. One voice was closer to the door than the others. It was Martha Harewood. She, of course, would be part of any group of staff that would speak to the family. She was Rachel's housemistress, possibly the member of staff who had come closest to Rachel for the period of time that she had been in Eliot House.

She was the member of staff who knew most about Rachel's family background. That was why, when Rose had decided to tell someone about the possible abuse that Rachel was facing from her mother's new boyfriend, she went to Martha Harewood.

Rose went to see the housemistress straight after her last class when she knew that Rachel had gone back to her room to get changed.

'Come in, Rose. What can I do for you?'

'I wanted to tell you something and it's pretty difficult

because I'm betraying a confidence but if I didn't think it was the right thing to do, if it wasn't better for the person concerned, I wouldn't be telling you.'

Rose stopped. She felt as though all the words in her mouth were in a jumble.

'You know that anything you tell me will be confidential.'

'But if a crime was being committed? It wouldn't be confidential then?'

'Ah, no. Then I could not hold a confidence. But if something criminal is involved then maybe you should tell.'

Rose hesitated.

'What is it, Rose? It's obviously upsetting you and I'm guessing it concerns your friend Rachel Bliss?'

Rose nodded. Martha waited. Eventually Rose spoke.

'It's about her mother's boyfriend. I think he's abusing her. Or at least he intends to abuse her. She's really upset about it and doesn't want to hurt her mum. His name's Robert and they're thinking of getting married and up to now Rachel has only had to put up with him for the odd weekend and part of the holidays but if they get married then he'll be a part of her life and she can't stand the thought of it . . .'

'Slow down. Slow down. Tell me slowly, all of it and be clear about what you're saying.'

Rose started again. Martha listened. She explained all the things that Rachel had told her. She described how

Rachel had to lock her door. She said how over the last few months it had got worse. Finally she told Martha about the visit home when her mother was ill and how Robert had come into her bedroom and then how he had told her he had bought her some new underwear. Martha kept her eyes on Rose and a kind of sadness seemed to register in her expression.

'Oh, Rose,' Martha said, and reached out to pat her hand.

'What will you do?' Rose said, suddenly fearful of what she'd said.

Martha got up and went to a filing cabinet. She opened the top drawer and Rose could see that it said *Year Eleven* on it. She sorted through the files for a moment before taking one out. Then she pulled the chair she had been sitting on a bit closer to Rose. She had Rachel's file in front of her. She was looking at it in a troubled way.

'Rose,' she said, 'I'm going to show you this. I'm actually not supposed to share the information with anyone but I think it's important that you see what is here.'

Rose frowned. Had this sort of thing happened to Rachel before? Had she been a victim of some kind of abuse in the past? Was Martha showing it to her so that she didn't have to feel bad about breaking a confidence?

Martha undid a plastic tag and removed the top sheet from Rachel's file. She handed it to Rose. Rose looked down at what was written there. She saw Rachel's name and address and then underneath the names of Margaret Bliss and Anthony Bliss. Beside them it said *Maternal Grandparents*.

'I don't understand,' she said.

There was nothing else on the sheet.

'Rachel lives with her grandparents. Her mother had her when she was seventeen and wanted to have her adopted. Her grandparents adopted her and the mother moved away and has not seen Rachel or her own parents since. I believe they heard through a friend of a friend that Rachel's mother is married and has a family of her own in the north. Rachel's grandparents are good people and love Rachel even though she has not always been an easy child to raise.'

Rose couldn't believe what she was hearing.

'For the first ten years of her life Rachel thought that Mr and Mrs Bliss were her parents but then they told her the truth and it upset her greatly. Maybe they were wrong to do that but still . . . From then on she battled with her grandparents. She has been at a number of schools and we thought she had settled when she came here. Then there was the dreadful suicide of poor Juliet Baker. When she became friends with you I thought that she had fallen on her feet. A good solid friend was what she needed.'

Rose couldn't speak. Her lips felt as though they would crack if she moved them.

'I can see you're upset but I felt it was important you

should know the truth. She's not a bad person, Rose, and she will grow out of this storytelling phase.'

Storytelling phase. She'd done it before. Of course, she had. She'd done it last summer when she told Rose that her half-sister had leukaemia. Rose had forgiven her then and she had promised never to do it again.

'We thought that she has been getting on OK over these last months. Her work, of course, could do with improvement but we were so pleased to see that she was in a steady friendship with you.'

Rose stood up. Martha looked concerned.

'Don't be angry with her, Rose. Go and talk it out with her. Maybe she'll open up to you. You and she have some things in common . . .'

Martha had stumbled on the last words and looked as if she wished she hadn't said them.

'What do you mean? What have we got in common?'

And then it came to Rose. They both had been abandoned by their mothers.

'No,' Rose said, shaking her head. 'No, there's no comparison. My mother is most probably dead because of her police work. She is a hero. She would never have left me of her own free will. She was abducted. How can you compare that to a seventeen-year-old girl who doesn't want her baby!'

'What I meant was you are both without mothers. That's all . . .'

182

But Rose turned away and walked out of Martha's rooms. She went straight along the corridor until she got to Rachel's door. She didn't knock – she barged in. Rachel was in her jeans and sweatshirt and looked as though she was starting to do some work. On her desk Rose could see the tiny jars of nail varnish lined up, their colours gaudy and gross.

'What's up?' Rachel said.

'You lied to me. You live with your gran and grandad. All that stuff about your dad's flat and your mum's new boyfriend, it was all a lie.'

Rachel looked away.

'Why?' Rose said.

Rachel shrugged.

'How could you? After last summer when you told me about your so-called sister? You said then that you'd never do it again. Why did you lie to me?'

Rachel made a show of choosing a jar of varnish. Then she took her time unscrewing the top. Rose waited for her to say *something*. She did not.

In exasperation Rose walked out. She headed for the stairs and out of the building, past the Year Sevens who were having a makeshift game of rounders. She walked to the furthest corner of the quad and sat down on a bench and put her face in her hands.

She was too angry to cry.

They'd been friends for over a year. Rose had been

loyal and she'd thought that Rachel was her true friend. They'd had their problems but still underneath it all she felt this extraordinary affection for her. Was it too much to say that she *loved* her? She was very still. She did, she loved her, but all the while Rachel had been lying her face off, creating a fiction out of her life. What kind of person was she?

The tears came then, hot enough to burn her skin.

It was finished. It was over.

She ignored Rachel. She went on with her work and wrote a letter to her grandmother asking if she could leave the school at the end of the year. The days were long and lonely but she held her head high and would not make eye contact with Rachel even though Rachel was often hanging around in the same bit of the quad as Rose or on a dining table nearby.

Then one day, weeks later, when she was having a low moment, she turned on her laptop to find the words *New message*.

It was from Joshua Johnson.

I'm trying to contact the Rose Smith who used to live in Brewster Road in Bethnal Green. If you are this person could you contact me? If not, sorry to have bothered you.

She stared at the email with disbelief.

Joshua? She said his name out loud, filled with a feeling of elation. Joshua Johnson, her stepbrother. She replied instantly.

Dear Joshua, yes, it's me. Your little stepsister, Rose. How are you? It's brilliant to hear from you!

Minutes later, she received a longer message.

Hi Rosie, at long last got hold of your email address (don't ask me how many emails I've sent to 'Rose Smith'). It's a long time since we spoke but I thought I'd contact you to tell you that I'm coming to London in September to go to college. I'll be living in Camden and I think that's not so far from where you live with your gran! Don't know if you'll be around or whether you even want to meet up and chat over old times. For years I've thought it was a shame that we lost touch. Now might be a good chance to get to know each other again. Joshua.

PS And it goes without saying that we could swap stories about Dad and Kathy. XXXX

She read it over, two, three times. Then she replied.

It felt like a new beginning.

The head teacher's door opened.

'You can come in now, Rose,' Mrs Abbott said.

Martha passed her, giving her arm a squeeze. In the head's office an elderly couple were sitting in the armchairs. There was a tray of tea and biscuits on the coffee table. Mrs Abbott introduced them.

'You're Rose?' the woman said. 'We heard a lot about you from Rachel. Thank you. You were a really good friend.'

Mrs Bliss had a solid square handbag on her lap and both her hands gripped the strap. Mr Bliss stood up and held his hand out for a shake.

'Whenever Rachel came home for the holidays she talked about you non-stop, didn't she, Tony?'

'She drove us mad. Rose Smith this, Rose Smith that!'

Rose frowned. She had no idea what to say to them. They were smiling at her in an encouraging way.

'I'm so sorry about her death,' Rose said.

The word *death* sat uncomfortably in the room.

'It's a terrible thing,' Mrs Bliss said, eventually, and then turned to her husband. 'She said she's sorry about Rachel's *accident*.'

'Dreadful,' Mr Bliss said.

'Miss Harewood told us that you knew that Rachel was our adopted daughter.'

'Yes,' said Rose.

'She was our pride and joy,' Mr Bliss said, sitting upright, brushing his trousers down with the side of his hand.

'Even if she didn't always think that was the case,' Mrs Bliss said, patting her husband's hand briefly before gripping the handle of the bag once more.

'Rachel was so upset when you left. She talked about you all last summer.'

Rose didn't know what to say. How to answer. How to make them feel any better.

'Let the girl go, dear,' Mr Bliss said.

He stood up and gave her a firm handshake and Mrs Bliss grabbed hold of her other hand and squeezed it briefly before sitting back down, hugging the handbag and sighing loudly.

Outside, Rose stood for a moment feeling the cooler air on her face. Then she went to the reception area and picked up her bag. She'd told Joshua to come up the drive and pick her up at the entrance but now she didn't want to wait around. She wanted to be away from the gloomy atmosphere of the building and the memories that it brought with it. She walked out of the door and along the drive. She'd meet Joshua as he drove towards her.

She wanted to go home to London.

EIGHTEEN

Joshua was late. She reached the end of the drive and expected to see him there but the lane was empty. She looked each way for the Mini to appear but it didn't. She checked the time; twenty past one. She rang his phone but it went straight to voicemail. She tried to remember what he said he was doing after he dropped her off earlier. Had he been delayed?

She knew what direction he was due to come from so she started to walk briskly along the lane. As she went she thought about Rachel Bliss's grandparents. They looked as though they were in their sixties. Had they known about the lies she told? Had they been offended that she made up stories about her family or had they blamed themselves because they'd waited so long to tell her the truth? Rachel had lived a lie with them for ten years. Had she been punishing them by making up a completely new family?

But why had Rachel punished *her* by lying?

She came to the end of the lane where the bus stop was. She looked north up the coast road for the Mini. She pulled out her phone to see if a message had arrived but there was nothing. It was 1.35. Where was Joshua Her bag felt heavier now and she pulled it across the road to the bus stop and sat on the small wooden seat, its edges crumbling, its fibres sticking up. From where she was she could see up the lane and for a considerable distance along the road. She'd be able to see the Mini when it came.

Then she could get away from here and put Rachel Bliss out of her mind once and for all.

After their friendship was over Rose and Rachel avoided each other. Rachel spent her time with other girls but Rose spent time alone. There were three things on her mind. To get the best grades on her exams. To persuade her grandmother to let her leave Mary Linton and go to a local high school. To get closer to Joshua.

Amid all of the revision she was amazed and delighted when there was a message from him. Many were long and detailed, telling her what had happened to him in the time that they had been separated. She replied, filling him in on her life although her emails seemed shorter, blunter than his.

It kept her going.

Her grandmother reluctantly agreed that she could

leave after her exams and look at local high schools for somewhere to do her senior year. Rose was delighted with this. It meant she could get away from school and Rachel Bliss and that she would be in London when Joshua moved there to go to university.

Maybe they could meet up soon. The thought gave her a thrill.

But she had to get her exams out of the way first and then pack her things up and leave Mary Linton School for Girls behind her.

Walking out of her last exam she felt exhilarated. Her wrist ached because of the fervour with which she had written her answers. She'd hardly paused to look at the other students or at the clock on the wall. She just kept writing, one paragraph after the other until she'd finished and then went on to the next question. When a voice said, *You have fifteen minutes left* she had looked up startled and then dipped her head back into her work once more until it was over.

It was a hot day and she went and sat in the quad feeling the late afternoon sun beating down on her face. She looked up at the building and knew that in a few days' time she would be leaving it for ever.

She was glad.

Then she saw Rachel coming round the corner. She kept her eyes fixed on a point on the building so that she didn't have to make eye contact or acknowledge her. But

Rachel walked straight towards her and sat next to her. Rose tensed herself. She did not want to have a conversation with Rachel but she could hardly ignore her at such close quarters.

'Finished?' Rachel said.

She nodded.

'I've still got another Classics paper.'

Rose didn't answer.

'There's something I wanted to tell you,' Rachel said, lowering her voice a little. 'I didn't know whether to or not but last Saturday I was in Cromer and I think I saw your mother.'

Rose turned slowly and stared at Rachel. Moments went by and she didn't utter a word. Then Rachel's eyes dropped and she made a sound clearing her throat.

'I was on the pier with some girls from Brontë. One of their parents took us out. We were larking about and I saw this couple standing in the corner. The woman was staring at me. We were in our own clothes but still she stared, not just at me but at the other girls as well and she looked so familiar. I thought I knew her, you know; maybe she'd worked in the school or in one of the shops in Holt or something. I didn't take much notice of her after that. I was too busy with the others but as I was walking away it came to me where I knew her from.'

Rose felt blank inside. As if she had no feelings at all.

'So I let the others walk on and I went back towards them. The woman and man were at the rail looking out to sea. They had their backs to me so I pretended to be tying up my lace and I heard the man say, *Are you all right? Did you think that one of those girls was Rose?*' Rachel went on breathlessly. 'That's when I knew. I mean you showed me enough pictures of your mother and, what with the man saying the name *Rose*, well, it just triggered the memory of those photos!'

Rose frowned.

'My mother's *dead*,' she said, turning away, trying to end the conversation.

'No! You said you were never sure. No one was really sure, you said that over and over and then last Saturday I saw her. Your mother. On the pier in Cromer. Don't you see? That's why she was looking closely at teenage girls. She was looking for you, Rose!'

Rachel was smiling, her eyes lit up with excitement. Rose could barely bring herself to speak. Her mouth was dry, her tongue grainy.

'So why did you wait until now to tell me?'

Rachel shifted her position on the bench.

'I wasn't going to tell you at all. Because, of course, I didn't want to upset you. But today I heard that you were leaving and I wanted you to know before you went. And the thing is, I know I shouldn't have done it, but I waited around a while and I followed the couple. They walked right along the front of Cromer and then went into one of the apartments? Like holiday lets?'

'You mean my mother was in Cromer on holiday?' Rose said, incredulous.

'I don't know. I'm just telling you that she was there. I recognised her and I heard the man say *Did you think one of those girls was Rose?* Those two things together made me think I should tell you.'

Rose looked away from Rachel. Of all the lies Rachel could tell why would she choose this one? There were many ways to hurt Rose but this was like sticking a knife in Rose's heart.

'Well?' Rachel said.

'I don't believe you.'

'I'm not lying. I mean, I know I haven't always told the complete truth in the past but I'm not lying about this!'

'Leave me alone.'

'I'm just trying to help you.'

'Go away, Rachel.'

There was silence and Rose turned back. Rachel's eyes were glistening with tears.

'It's true,' she whispered.

'Get out of my sight,' Rose said and closed her eyes.

After a few moments she heard movement and footsteps and when she opened her eyes again Rachel was gone and it was just the sun beating down, scorching her skin. At that point Rose felt a flood of anguish, her chest contracting, her throat awash.

Her mother in Cromer, within arm's reach, a whisper away.

How much she wished that was true.

Now it was two o'clock and there was no sign of Joshua. A bus had come and gone, some Mary Linton girls giggling and laughing as they got off and headed across the lane back towards school. The driver idled at the stop to see whether she wanted to get on. She shook her head and wondered what to do.

It wasn't like Joshua to not turn up. Not without ringing her or sending an email. There was no signal here so she would have to walk back to the school building and see if she had an email from him. If not then she could find the number of the White Rose and ring it to see if Joshua was there. Most probably he'd mislaid his phone. That might be the entire reason for his lateness. During his travels to see the guy from the parish council he must have left it somewhere and at that very moment he was retracing his steps and looking for it. There was nothing else to do but to go back to school.

Back in the school reception she went over to the waiting area and got her laptop out. She waited for it to load up, then she looked up the number of the White Rose and rang it but she was told that he had checked out of his room after eleven.

Rose didn't know what to do. She looked at the time. It was 2.35. She'd give Joshua until three and then she'd decide what to do.

At three she sent an email.

Josh, I don't know why you're late. I'm guessing you've lost your phone and are looking for it. I'm going to wait until 3.30, then I'm going to get a cab into Stiffkey and look for you. If we miss each other that's where I'll be. Rose xxxx

She waited until 3.30 and then phoned for a cab. A couple of girls she knew from Eliot House were passing by and she asked one of them to take her bag and laptop up to Martha Harewood's rooms for safe keeping. She didn't want to carry it round with her. She'd go to the White Rose and see what had happened to Joshua. Even though he had checked out he might still go back there. Maybe the car had broken down somewhere.

He would turn up, she was sure. Then they could pick up her stuff and drive back to London. She thought this over and over but inside there was a niggle of worry.

Joshua was so reliable. Where was he?

NINETEEN

The driver turned into the car park of the White Rose and Rose got out and paid him. She went straight into the inn. It was just after four o'clock but there were still people eating Sunday lunch. The inn's bar was busy and the place was hot, the smell of cooked food strong, inviting. The barman was brusque when she asked about Joshua. He'd not seen him since he checked out. He pointed out a man sitting in the far corner of the bar. She was flustered but she went across and said who she was. It was Colin Crabtree, the man who Joshua had arranged to see. 'He never turned up, my dear. Around twelve he said. I had my documents ready but he never came,' he said.

She headed for the exit.

Outside it was getting dark, the sky charcoal grey. She walked away from the pub in the direction that they'd travelled in the car that morning. There were some lights on in houses but they were set back and beyond them just swathes of shadowy farmland. She'd been living in

London for months now. She was used to constant noise and light and movement everywhere so the depth of quiet seemed unnatural. She had a horrible feeling inside. Joshua had dropped her off at the end of the school drive about half past ten. That gave him plenty of time to go back to the inn, get his stuff together and go and see the man from the parish council.

He checked out of the inn soon after eleven.

Where had he gone then?

She did not know what to do. The narrow road stretched away into the darkness. She walked on, keeping to the side. There was no traffic. When she passed the last village light the road ahead was almost black. She went on, carefully stopping once to stand flat up against the side of the road when the lights of a car showed. It lit up the hedgerow and the road and for a moment she could see everything. Then it was gone and it seemed darker than before. She walked slowly and reached the lane that had the sign for *Beach*.

Had he gone back there? Back to the cottage?

She would walk up to the beach car park. If there was no sign of his car then she would come back to the pub and decide what to do. She turned and felt a blast of cold air coming from the mudflats. The lane ahead was silent and she felt uneasy walking along it. There was light from the moon, though, and she could see the high hedges that cut the houses off from prying eyes. She made herself go briskly along it, looking from side to side, listening for any sounds of people or cars or stray animals. Up ahead she could see where the houses ended and the campsite began.

The car park came into view and she could see the Mini. She felt a spurt of relief. At last. She quickened her step. The mudflats beyond were vast and silent so that the car looked tiny, moored on the edge of a flat brown sea. She hoped more than anything that Joshua was sitting inside. Even though the lights were off and it looked abandoned she hoped that Joshua had somehow fallen asleep in it and that she could wake him up and they could laugh it off, pick her stuff up from school and head back to London.

But when she got to the car she could see that it was empty.

And locked.

She looked around, with some vague hope of seeing Joshua appear from the coastal path that they'd been on that morning, but there was nothing. The place was completely deserted, just her and the Mini.

The wind washed through her and she shivered.

There was only one place Joshua could have gone. Back to the cottage. She remembered him that morning opening the top padlock and saying, *If I had a crowbar I could get the other padlock off and look inside.* She had been offhand about the whole thing and had angered him so that he was quiet and offish on the drive back to Mary Linton. Had he been so upset about her dismissal of the cottage that he had gone back there in order to prove something to her? And to himself?

What could have happened to him? Was he hurt? Had he had some kind of accident? The thought of it made her chew anxiously at her lip.

She rubbed her hands together. Her gloves were back in her rucksack. She looked down the lane that led to the village, wondering whether to seek help. It would be a sensible thing to do. She glanced over at the coastal path that they'd used that morning. It was inky black and she didn't have a torch. What should she do?

She should go back to the inn.

But if Joshua was hurt? Lying on the ground? Freezing cold? Hadn't she wasted enough time already?

She walked towards the coastal path. She would go and find him. It was a ten- or fifteen-minute walk. She had her phone to call for the emergency services if needed. She shoved her hands far into her pockets and walked on. She looked up, grateful for the moonlight, and trod carefully along the rutted path, her eyes getting used to the dark. After a few moments she felt a little more confident. It wasn't so bad. It wasn't as wild as she had thought. It was just a path in the country in the early evening. She counted the steps, twenty, forty, sixty-six, a hundred and twenty.

She heard a noise up ahead. It was the sound of an

engine starting. She stopped and listened. From somewhere in front she could hear a car. She had no idea how far away it was. She looked into the darkness as far ahead as she could. She strained her eyes to see if there was movement but all she could see were swathes of dark blue and grey punctuated by shapes of bushes or trees. If there was a car on the lane then she should see the lights no matter how far ahead it was.

But there were no lights – just the low rumble of the engine as it seemed to move closer. She had no reason to be scared of it and yet there was a pinprick of fear in her chest. She felt her shoulders rounding so that she was crouched instead of walking straight. It was ridiculous. She stood erect and tried to pull herself together. It was the dark that was spooking her. She forced herself on, one footstep after another. The car noise was coming from somewhere over to her left, towards the land not the mudflats. She expected to see it at any minute but the noise rumbled on as if it was twisting and turning.

It could be miles away. The place was so silent that any noise might sound as though it was close.

She came to the spot where they'd turned off towards the cottage and looked hard. The noise got louder. The car was coming from that direction, from somewhere near the cottage. She couldn't see it yet but it was getting closer. She stepped behind a clump of bushes and waited. The sound came nearer and when she peeked out she could see the shape of it, silver grey, the moonlight glancing off it as it came forward.

Why did it have no lights on?

She stepped further back into the bushes. She felt the foliage prodding into her neck as she waited for the car to reach her and turn on to the coast path lane and back towards Stiffkey. She looked again and saw that the car was, in fact, an SUV. It went slowly, dipping up and down at the ruts in the path. Eventually it edged past her. She saw one man in the driving seat. That was all.

As soon as it was out of sight she went down the path towards the cottage. She kept to the side of the lane, stepping quietly, almost holding her breath.

Who was the man in the SUV? And why was he visiting the cottage on exactly the same weekend as she and Joshua? Had he seen Joshua at the cottage? Had someone else from the village seen Joshua and informed the owner? Did he think that Joshua was trespassing? Had he come to check on his property?

Rose straightened up because something had occurred to her. Had Joshua been at the cottage when the SUV had come along? Perhaps Joshua had hidden to keep out of the way of the owner and had to stay put until the owner left. Possibly that's why he hadn't picked her up but was stranded in some way, hiding from the man in the SUV. It didn't really make much sense but it was an explanation of sorts.

She went carefully and slowly down the lane. When the lane opened out and she could see the shape of the cottage she began to feel anxious again.

She stopped in her tracks.

She could see a tiny light in the darkness.

It was at the side of the cottage and it only took her a moment to work out what it was. A lit cigarette. A man was standing smoking. He was side on and she could make out his shape but she couldn't see his face. She stood very still, not wanting him to see her there. A few seconds later, he coughed and the cigarette was thrown away. She could see it burning on the ground.

The man said something. It sounded as though he was swearing. He walked away from the cottage to the far edge of the plot and turned his back. He seemed to be static in front of a hedge and then she realised that he was peeing. She moved stealthily towards the cottage and edged along the wall. She stood by one of the boarded-up windows.

Now what?

She looked at the window. Wooden planks were nailed over it. Then she saw a strip of light shining through.

There was a light *inside* the cottage.

She tried to look through the gap between the planks but it was too narrow.

Then came the tinkling sound of a ringtone. For a second she froze, completely still, because she thought it was hers. But it was a different tone and it came from the other side of the cottage. She listened while the man answered it. His voice was low and she tried to make out what he was saying. She crept back to the corner of the building and looked out. He was talking and gesticulating but his words were incomprehensible. Then she did hear something. 'I'm losing signal,' he said loudly, but his words blurred again and she realised that he was speaking in another language. She listened hard. It sounded eastern European. He spoke rapidly and then suddenly stopped and swore in English and said, 'No signal!' She edged out as he marched up the lane. He was trying to get some phone reception. She heard him say, 'Lev! Lev!' as if the person on the other end of the line couldn't hear.

The name Lev rang a bell. She thought for a moment.

Lev Baranski, the son of Viktor Baranski, the man whose photo was in the notebook they got from Frank Richards. Joshua had gone to his restaurant in South Kensington a couple of days before. *Lev*. Was that what she'd heard? Or was she imagining it?

He could have said *Les*.

She watched as he walked away from the cottage. He merged into the darkness but she could still hear his voice. Perhaps he'd found enough reception and was staying put. She took small steps along the side of the cottage until she came to the corner and went round the back. There was another boarded-up window there and a door beyond but like the front door it had padlocks on it.

She went back to the window. She felt around the boards. They were nailed firmly but the corner of one was weathered and dry and when she grabbed the wood slivers of it peeled off in her hand. She picked up a broken tile from the ground and used it to gouge away at the plank until it came loose. Then she was able to insert the corner of the tile in between the plank and the window. She levered the tile back and forward until she felt the wood move a few centimetres.

She stopped, afraid of anyone hearing her or noticing anything from inside the cottage. When no sound came she continued working the tile behind the wood until a chunk came off and a small hole the size of a golf ball appeared.

She listened carefully for any sound from round the front of the cottage. There was nothing. She couldn't even hear the man talking on his phone any more. Most likely he'd come back up the lane and was standing outside again. Was he waiting for the man in the SUV to return? Was that man *Lev*?

She stepped towards the hole in the boards and looked through. There was a table, a couple of chairs, a stool. On the bare floorboards, near the door, was a powerful torch that gave the room an eerie light which faded out at the corners.

Just then the front door opened and the man came into the room. Rose jumped back from the eyehole. When she heard him speak she looked through again. He was talking to someone who she couldn't see.

'You think it funny to come to Lev's restaurant and make joke? You think Lev Baranski does not know who you are? You think he will sit by while you disrespect his father. You wait till he is here. Then see. Then see you disrespect him.'

Rose breathed in sharply. He had to be talking to Joshua.

The man walked a couple of steps and then bent over.

'You, Johnson boy. You make joke? You laugh at this!'

Rose clenched her hands as she saw the man grab something and pull it across the floor. Then he aimed his foot and kicked it. She closed her eyes with shock. There was a yelping sound and she looked again to see the front door slam and in the middle of the room, lying on the floor, was Joshua.

Her stomach dropped at the sight of him.

Joshua was tied up, his hands behind his back. There was masking tape across his mouth but she could still see his face twisted with pain.

TWENTY

Her mind whirling, Rose stared at Joshua lying on the floor of the cottage. The Russian man knew who he was. He knew his name was Johnson. A feeling of nausea came over her and she bent over as if to be sick. When she turned back to the eyehole Joshua had wriggled himself round so that she could only see his back. The Russian man had not come back in. He must be standing out the front.

She pulled at the wood to see if she could make the hole bigger. She picked up the tile she'd been using and began to dig furiously at the wood again. Then she stopped, realising the stupidity of it. What was she going to do? Chip her way into the cottage? And even if she managed to lever off enough wood, what then?

A feeling of weakness overwhelmed her.

Joshua had been right. About the cottage and about Viktor Baranski. She had dismissed the idea and had even begun to think that Frank Richards' notebooks were some fantasy project which had nothing to do with her mum and Brendan. But she was wrong. In some inexplicable way it was all linked to their disappearance.

Joshua had gone to the restaurant in Kensington and now Lev Baranski's man was at the cottage in Stiffkey. He had tied Joshua up and attacked him. Lev Baranski was on his way to show Joshua that he couldn't *disrespect* his father.

She had to *do* something.

She pulled her mobile out of her pocket. She wanted to ring 999 but then she would have to *speak*. The Russian man was only round the other side of the building. He would hear her, she was sure. Was it possible to send a text to 999? No, stupid. And in any case what would she say? How would she explain where they were? A cottage somewhere *near* Stiffkey?

She crept along the back of the building. Was there some other way to get in? The back door was firmly padlocked and the window beyond it was boarded-over. The only entrance seemed to be the front door. But while the Russian man was out there how could she get to Joshua?

And what would happen when Lev Baranski got here?

A grim feeling settled on her chest. Skeggsie had said that Lev Baranski's father had been murdered six years before by the Russian secret service. How did this relate to her mum and Brendan? Now Lev, his son, had recognised Joshua in the restaurant in Kensington. But how? Unless he had had some interest in Joshua, pictures of him. Why would he have done that? And why was he coming to Stiffkey to the very cottage that had been marked on Brendan's map?

There were too many questions she couldn't answer. The most important thing was to get to Joshua and free him. Possibly the SUV was going to pick up Lev Baranski? Not all the way to Kensington? Somewhere nearby perhaps. Possibly he was sitting in a plush hotel while other people did his dirty work.

She was gripping her phone.

Do something, Rose, she thought, *do something!*

She looked down at the screen to see the words *Low Battery*. She closed her eyes with despair. How could she have let her battery get so run down? How could she? She had maybe enough power to make one call for help. But to whom? She could text Skeggsie. He could call the police for them. But what if he was still in bed ill, or working on some animation, transfixed on creating something. What if he didn't pick up his messages for hours? She couldn't chance it.

She looked at her mobile and remembered Frank Richards.

When he gave his phone number to her, scribbled on the back of an envelope, he'd said, *I'll never answer this number but you can leave a message for me and I will get it.*

He said he would help her. Now she needed him.

She stood by the window and used the light from the eyehole to stab out a text.

I'm in trouble. Baranski has Josh in the Stiffkey cottage. Help me.

If Joshua was right, if the notebooks did link up with her mum and Brendan, if the Stiffkey cottage had something to do with it, then Frank Richards (whatever his real name was) would know what she was referring to. She pressed *Send*. The words *No network coverage* immediately appeared and she swore silently, remembering the Russian man walking up the lane to use his mobile.

The message she needed to send was stuck in limbo and wouldn't go anywhere until there was a signal.

She looked through the eyehole again. Joshua was lying in the same place. The man had not come back in. If she could just let Joshua know that she was there. She stepped back and felt round with her foot. She picked up three small stones and placed one in the eyehole and then gave it a shove. It dropped on to the cottage floor. She waited but Joshua did not look round. Then she dropped the second one. He must have heard it because he moved his shoulder and tried to look back. She shoved the third stone through and it made a louder noise than the other two. She watched, holding her breath, as Joshua edged himself closer to the rear of the room and with an almighty effort flipped himself over so that he was facing the window and the stones.

Could he see her?

She got another stone and pushed it through.

He began to nod his head as if to send a signal.

He knew someone was at the window. Maybe he sensed that it was her. Now she had to do something to get him out and she had to do it before Lev Baranski got here. She walked quickly and quietly to the corner of the cottage and then along the side. She looked out and saw the Russian man further up the lane. A distant ringtone sounded and he answered his phone. She listened for a few moments. The tone of his voice was different; he sounded as if he was talking to a friend rather than to his boss. He began to walk forward. He was trying to hold on to the signal.

She willed him to keep going, to get as far up the lane as possible. He stopped but the conversation went on and she realised that this was the only chance she was going to have to get into the cottage.

She stepped out of her hiding place and walked sideways with her back to the wall until she got to the front door, previously padlocked top and bottom but now open. She put her hand on the door and pushed it back. She stepped inside the cottage and closed the door again.

She turned round and there was Joshua on the floor.

She didn't speak, she just rushed across and knelt down beside him. His hands and feet had been tied with masking tape and his mouth gagged. His hands were icy. She pulled at the stuff round his wrists but it stayed firm. He turned his head to her and was tilting his chin up. She looked at the strip of tape across his mouth and felt herself go weak. If she pulled it off it would hurt him badly. He saw her reluctance and nodded his head more decisively. She edged up the corner of the tape and held it firmly. Joshua closed his eyes and she took a deep breath and ripped it off his mouth. He seemed to rock back with the pain but he didn't make a sound. With tears in her eyes she patted the sore skin with her hand. He shook his head, backing away.

He whispered, 'My bag, penknife, front pouch.'

She looked round and saw, in the corner by a cupboard, Joshua's rucksack lying at an angle as if it had been kicked there. She went across to it and pulled out a Swiss Army knife. With trembling fingers she opened out a blade and a series of other sharp attachments came too. Isolating the blade she began to chop at the masking tape on Joshua's hands. Then she began to slice through the tape round his feet.

All this time neither of them said a word.

Finally Joshua was free and he got to his feet and picked up his bag. Then he stepped towards her and pulled her into a fierce hug.

'Rosie,' he whispered in her ear.

He kissed the side of her face and she closed her eyes, the relief of having freed him making her feel light-headed. He stood back from her and looked her up and down.

'You OK? Not hurt?'

She nodded and he went to the door and pushed it open a few centimetres. The Russian was still on the phone in the lane. He had his back to them.

They crept out of the cottage and closed the door behind them. Joshua headed in the direction of the outbuilding where the boat was. Rose followed him, glancing round to make sure the Russian was staying put. Joshua pointed to a clump of trees across open ground. It was a fair distance, maybe a kilometre, but it was the only place to hide on the otherwise flat land. Rose nodded in agreement. All the time they could hear the man talking on his mobile in a companionable way. They got to the outbuilding and paused. There was enough moonlight to see a path across the fields. Joshua went first and waited until Rose was next to him before making to climb the stile.

But Rose pulled him back.

In the distance there was the slow rumble of a car engine. The Russian man must have heard it too because he stopped talking abruptly and there was absolute silence except for the motor approaching from the coastal path.

Rose looked fearfully at Joshua.

How long before the car arrived and they returned to the cottage and found it empty? Would there be time for her and Joshua to run across the fields to the copse? Would they not be seen in the moonlight?

She grabbed Joshua and pulled him close and whispered into his ear, 'Behind the boat.'

He nodded and they slipped into the outbuilding. There was still no sign of the Russian. Maybe he'd walked further up the lane to meet the car. Joshua went across to the boat. The tarpaulin was hanging down, almost covering the wooden struts that held the boat in place. At the corner were some wooden crates and he moved them one by one so that there was a space where they could creep under the hull and round the other side against the wall. He pushed Rose to go first and then followed. The space at the corner was small but when Joshua pulled the tarpaulin down they were covered up. Rose edged back as far as she could into the corner.

She was terrified.

She could feel Joshua's breath like fire on her neck. His arms were in front of him and she sought out one of his hands and held it. He placed his other hand over the top of hers and squeezed it gently.

Together they sat still and silent and waited.

TWENTY-ONE

The boat smelled of brine and fish and damp. The paint was peeling and the wood, centimetres from her face, was heavy with mildew.

Rose's chest lifted and settled, lifted and settled.

If they could just stay there, like that. The wall behind them, the boat camouflaging them. Possibly the Russians would think that, somehow, Joshua had got free and had run as far away as he could. They may even give up and leave.

The engine noise of the SUV came closer until it seemed to be outside, metres away from where they were sitting. Then it stopped. For a few seconds there wasn't a sound, then the doors of the vehicle opened. She heard voices, mostly in Russian, and the sound of walking on the rough path up to the front door of the cottage.

Then there was a shout and a lot of noise; heavy footsteps walking swiftly here and there and doors banging from inside the cottage. Moments later someone restarted the car engine and swung it round, kicking up pebbles from beneath it. There was shouting and people running past the outbuilding and back again. A voice came from far away, perhaps from the direction of the fields where they had been headed. Then it came back as though whoever it was had run so far and was now on their way back.

Rose was stiller than she'd ever been in her life. The only thing that was moving was the beat of her heart. It was at her very centre and pulsed rapidly while her body was still as a corpse. Then suddenly everything outside went quiet and she listened hard. Joshua tensed beside her. Would it have been better to take their chances and run across the field?

The silence was filled with intent.

She heard a footstep outside the outbuilding. A single footfall. As if someone was moving stealthily towards them. The smell of the boat was making Rose feel sick. She felt bile at the back of her throat.

The door of the outbuilding creaked open.

It would only be minutes before they found them.

She gagged silently, letting go of Joshua's hand to cover her mouth. She felt him tense, his muscles hardening. Her hand flopped and touched the ground. It was slimy and damp and her fingers felt something lying in the corner by the wall. It was a chain of some sort and she grabbed on to it, closing her hand over it.

The sound of voices began, talking rapidly. Through the tarpaulin she saw the beam of a torch swinging across the walls of the outbuilding.

Was there any possibility that they would just look in the building? That they would discount the parcelled up boat? But this thought was dismissed as she saw hands on the tarpaulin and then sensed a whoosh of air as it was rudely pulled to the side, leaving them exposed to the beam of the torch and the faces beyond.

A great guffaw of laughter came from the men.

'What a smell!' one of them said in English.

Another voice, quieter, calmer, spoke.

'Get them out of there.'

Then there were hands pulling at her feet and legs, sliding her out of the hiding place and dropping her unceremoniously on the floor of the outbuilding. Joshua followed but he immediately stood up, squaring his shoulders. The man who had kicked him earlier gave a grin as though he was looking forward to something. It made Rose's head feel weak.

'Mikey, bring them outside.'

There were three men. One of them had walked out ahead of the others. Rose felt one man grab her arm and hoist her to her feet and lead her out into the night air. The other pulled Joshua. The SUV was in front of the cottage, its headlights blazing, lighting up the whole area. The man thrust her towards the cottage and let her go.

She leant up against the wall, glad to have something at her back. She looked down at herself. In the light she could see her jeans were damp from the floor of the outbuilding. One of her hands was clenched. She was still holding the chain she had found behind the boat. Her fist looked fused, as if it would never uncurl.

The men went quiet.

'I have message for you.'

The man at the SUV spoke with authority and Rose thought he was probably Lev Baranski, the son of the man in the photo.

'You tell your father I will never stop looking for him.'

All the men were staring at them.

'My father is dead,' Joshua said.

Lev Baranski shook his head. 'I knew, all these years, that he was not dead. I knew where you were, what you were doing. I made it my business to know. I waited. One day you came to me. Then I knew it was time to find you, to talk to you. Because I know it will only be a matter of time before you will show me where your father is. He's not here. I can see that. So I'm just giving you and your girlfriend a message. Tell him I will be coming for him.'

'I can't tell him anything. I haven't seen him for five years.'

'You will see him. One day. Be sure to let him know that I have not forgotten my father's death and I never will.'

There was silence. The mention of Viktor Baranski seemed to quieten the men who all looked at the ground as if they were at some kind of memorial service. Then, after what seemed like a moment's reflection, the man who had kicked Joshua earlier pulled something out of his pocket and pointed it at him. A knife flicked out, startling Rose.

'You want I should rough him. Hurt him?' he said to Lev Baranski.

Joshua moved towards Rose. He held out one arm as if to divide her off from what was taking place.

'Just a little message for father? An eye? An ear?'

Lev Baranski stared at both of them. He seemed to be considering it. Rose's legs felt liquid as if they might pour away at any moment.

'No,' he said. 'Not this time. This time I want him to go to his father and say that Lev Baranski wants to see him. No more, no less. Next time, though . . .'

He paused and looked at Rose for the first time. She held his eyes.

'Next time not so lucky.'

He turned round and got into the SUV. The men with him stood for a moment and stared menacingly at Rose and Joshua and then one of them got into the vehicle. The other put his hand in his pocket and pulled out something and threw it at Joshua. It skidded along the ground and landed by his foot. It was a mobile phone. Joshua dipped down and picked it up. The man got into the SUV and it reversed and swung round. Keeping its lights on this time, it made its way up the lane faster than it had come, see-sawing over the bumpy terrain.

Rose and Joshua stood very still watching it go. Only when its rear lights disappeared did Rose find herself sliding down the wall, hitting the ground with a bump and breaking into shuddering sobs.

'Rosie, Rosie,' Joshua whispered, sitting down beside her.

She looked at him. In the dark she couldn't see his expression but she put her arms up to him and pulled him into a hug. He hugged her back, making shushing sounds and after a few moments she stopped crying and leant back against the wall, exhausted.

'We should get out of here,' he said, his voice still in a whisper.

'In case they change their minds?'

'I don't think they will. But you're freezing and so am I.'

She nodded and made a shaky attempt to get to her feet, rubbing her eyes with the back of her hand. He helped her and tried to hold the hand that was closed tight.

'What's this?'

She opened her palm to show the chain she had picked up from behind the boat. It was clunky, an identity bracelet, one half of the chain missing. It looked old-fashioned and had something engraved on it but she couldn't make out the word.

'I found it,' she said.

'My bag's in the boathouse,' he said. 'You stay here and I'll go and get it.'

'No, I'm coming with you! Then we go, right? Get away from here?'

He nodded and she followed him to the boathouse. She made sure the door was wide open and stood by it, not wanting to go in again. She kept looking back to the lane and listening intently for any sound of the car engine coming back. Joshua got down on his knees and edged under the hull of the boat to where they had been hiding. She waited, her eyes adjusting to the interior. A wash of grey light poured into the boathouse. Joshua was backing out from under the hull when she looked up and saw the side of the boat, visible now because the Russians had pulled back the tarpaulin.

'Oh, my!' she said, astonished at what she saw.

'What?' Joshua said.

The two of them stood opposite the boat and looked at the remains of the painted name it had been given.

The word *Butterfly* stared back at them.

Joshua gasped and walked forward, putting his hand out to trace the letters as if he couldn't quite believe what he was seeing. He took out his phone and pressed the keys so that it lit up for a second, illuminating the sign and Rose could see that the boat had once been dark blue and the lettering yellow.

'I don't believe this,' he said.

Neither did she. The boat, the cottage, the notebooks. All of it was too much for her. She felt the chain still in her hand and took out her own mobile phone to get some light and remembered that the battery was running low. She held the name plate from the chain under it and pressed it to get a last bit of light from it. The words *Message Sent* came on to the screen.

For a second she was puzzled and then she remembered the text she had written to Frank Richards. She had called out for help but the message hadn't gone. Now it had finally found a signal and transmitted. Too late to be of any use to them.

She held the chain in front of the screen and pressed, hoping there was just enough battery to see the inscription on the nameplate. It lit up for a second then went black. She pressed a few more times but her battery had run out completely. It didn't matter, though. She had just made out the inscription.

The name on the identity bracelet was Вайктор.

A Russian name.

They got into the car quickly and shut out the cold night air. Rose was shivering and Joshua was blowing on his hands.

'Let's get out of here,' he said, starting the car.

In moments they were driving away, turning out of the lane with the sign that said *Beach*. Joshua drove past the White Rose and kept going. He drove without speaking. The heater was running but the air seemed lukewarm. Rose looked at the time: 6.07 p.m. Was it just two hours before that she had been dropped off at the pub, looking for Joshua?

As they drove she thought about the things that had happened. Lev Baranski thought that Brendan had something to do with his father's death. Hadn't Skeggsie said that the Russian secret service killed Viktor Baranski? Could it be that their parents had become involved in a national security matter? Had they given information to the Russian secret service which enabled them to kill Viktor? Was that why Lev Baranski wanted to see Brendan?

Something occurred to her as she thought about this. Lev said he wanted to see Brendan. Lev had been interested only in Joshua. Was it possible that it was only Brendan who was involved in national security and that her mother had been sucked into something she had nothing to do with?

When the road widened out Joshua pulled over and parked the car up on the verge. He took his seat belt off and so did she. He sat very still as if trying to calm himself. The engine was still running, the temperature in the car finally heating up.

'After I dropped you off I went back and checked out of the inn. I was loading my stuff in the back of Skeggsie's car when I saw this crowbar there. You know Skeggsie. He probably had it in his car for protection or something. I made a snap decision to go and find out what was in the cottage. I got there, I unlocked the top padlock and jemmied the door. I went inside. I had a look around. You could see for yourself there wasn't much to find and as I came out this SUV was coming down the lane and I wondered whether it was some local people. I was going to ask questions but then the guy from the restaurant in South Kensington got out of the passenger door. It took a few moments for me to realise who he was.'

'He followed you here all the way from London?'

'I don't know. I think he must have. They must have recognised me at the restaurant and maybe he was hanging around outside the flat. He saw me getting into the car and followed, not knowing that I was going a long distance. Him and another guy. Anyway, the two of them just walked over and took me by surprise. I put up a fight of sorts but I got punched and I went down on the floor. Then they wrapped my hands and feet with the tape and then put it over my mouth.'

'You must have been there for hours.'

'They called Lev and he had to get to Norfolk. One of them drove off a while before you came – probably to pick Lev up and bring him here.'

'What do we do with all this?' she said.

'I don't know. I need to talk to Skeggs.'

She was momentarily stung. Why couldn't he talk to her?

Joshua seemed to register what he'd said.

'I just need his computers and know-how. After this we've got a whole new lot of information to explore.'

They were quiet, the heater making a low noise in the car. Outside it was pitch-dark. No other car had passed them for ages. Joshua's hand went up to his lips and he seemed to cup the skin around there. Rose pulled at his arm and made him turn round to face her. Across his mouth was an angry red welt.

'That looks so sore.'

He dismissed it with a wave of his hand.

She lifted her fingers and went to touch the skin but he shrank back. She got hold of his sweatshirt, though, and pulled him nearer.

'When I saw you tied up I didn't know what was going to happen. I thought . . . I don't know what I thought I was so frightened.'

'I was worried, Rosie. I didn't want you involved in anything dangerous . . .'

He put his hand on the back of her neck. She turned towards him. His touch was warm, his fingers stroking her skin beneath her hair. If anything had happened to him what would she have done? She looked up at him, at his worried expression and a surge of emotion went through her. She wanted to kiss his bruised mouth gently, without hurting him. The thought of it made her weak in the pit of her stomach.

He caught her eyes and they stared at each other for what seemed like a long time. He went to say something but stopped.

'What?' she whispered.

He shook his head.

His eyes dropped away and he pulled his hand back.

'As long as you're all right, Rosie,' he said.

She nodded, her neck cold from where his hand had been.

She sat back in the passenger seat, dazed.

'What shall we do now?'

'Go home?'

She nodded. 'My stuff's at the school, though. We need to pick it up.'

He started the car and they drove back towards Mary Linton. He put the CD player on and music filled the car. Usually it would have cheered her up but she felt it pounding in her ears and she longed for the silence of the mudflats. As they passed through the school gates and went along the drive, Rose put her fingers up to her mouth. There she felt the kiss that hadn't happened.

When they pulled up outside the main entrance she saw Joshua's hand gingerly touch his mouth again.

'Come into the building. There's first aid and I can get you a couple of painkillers. We can have a sandwich or something before we drive home.'

He nodded, cut the engine and got out and they both walked towards the entrance. He looked terrible, battered and shaky. He lagged behind her and after a minute she waited, took his arm and pulled him on into the building.

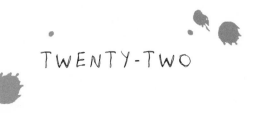

TWENTY-TWO

Martha Harewood wouldn't let them drive back to London.

She clucked and fussed over them. She got the first-aid kit out and tried to clean up Joshua's face. She asked a hundred questions but Rose just told her that they'd been walking on the coastal path and misjudged the time, eventually stumbling in the dark. Martha took them to one of the small kitchens and made scrambled eggs and toast. She shooed off the inquisitive girls who were milling round wondering what had happened. She arranged for Joshua to stay in the staff quarters and told Rose to go back to her old room and have an early night. Rose watched as Martha led Joshua off down the corridor. She hadn't been able to argue with her and was glad that Martha had made the decision for them.

She wanted to go to bed.

She went back to the room she'd left that morning. She put her phone on charge and remembered for a moment the message she'd sent to Frank Richards. It made her feel foolish now and she wondered whether he would get it and wonder what on earth it was about.

Her bedding was still on the floor where she'd pulled it off. She didn't bother to remake the bed or even get undressed. She replaced the pillows and got under the duvet. Her hip felt sore. She must have banged it on the ground while she was being flung around by the Russian man, Mikey. She turned the lights off. There was noise along the corridors, the sound of feet passing, girls talking, laughing.

It didn't bother her.

She was too tired to care.

She sank into a deep sleep.

When she woke the room was silent and black save for a finger of grey light that poked through the curtains. She looked at the clock. It was 0.07 She'd slept for four or more hours. She was drowsy and a heavy feeling came over her as the events of the previous evening resurfaced. She felt a moment's fright at what might have happened at the cottage. It was as if they had been teetering on the edge of a dark hole. She remembered Mikey standing with his knife. *Just a little message for father! An eye! An ear!* And for a second she felt sick again. She sat up and made herself breathe slowly.

She tried to lie down again but felt something sticking into her side. She put her hand in her pocket and pulled out the identity bracelet that she had found. She let her fingers trace the letters Вайктор.

Why was it there beside the boat, *Butterfly?*

Did the boat belong to Brendan? Did the cottage belong to him? Joshua had been sure it did. Was he also right that her mother and Brendan had been transferred from Cold Cases to national security? Instead of investigating old unsolved murders they now worked for the British secret service? Was that why Lev Baranski blamed Brendan for his father's death? *You tell your father I will never stop looking for him.*

These things kept going round and round in her head.

She was not going to sleep. She stood up and walked across the dark room, stretching her arms out, feeling her joints crack. She went over to the window and looked out through the gap in the curtains. She stared into the night. The dark had obliterated the usual view, the grass, the quad, the lake. She went to close the curtains tight but something was niggling her. She peered out, not really sure what it was.

Then she saw it; a tiny light moving through the grounds. She blinked but it was gone and she thought she had imagined it. Seconds later, though, it was there again, a dull glow in the blackness. She watched for a few seconds and her eyes began to make some sense of it. It was a torch. Someone was walking through the grounds.

In the direction of the boathouse.

She watched carefully, the light growing dimmer and dimmer and then somewhere round the boathouse it went off.

Someone going to the boathouse. Just after midnight.

She sat down on the bed.

It was nothing to do with her if some girls were out in the middle of the night. After five minutes of staring into the dark room, though, she sighed and stood up. It wasn't her business but maybe if someone had followed Rachel Bliss out then she might not have died. She pulled on her coat and went quietly out of her room and down the stairs, taking care not to make any sound. On the ground floor the school was completely still. Dotted here and there were night lights. There was the sound of a radio or television from further along a corridor, most likely one of the housemistresses on a night shift. She doubled back towards the classrooms and walked quickly past the language labs and the science block and then made a turn down a corridor that said *Staff Only*.

She passed the laundry block and headed for the side door that led out to one of the pick-up and delivery areas. She opened the door. The cold hit her. She clicked the snib on the lock so that the door wouldn't close behind her. She wondered why Rachel had needed Molly to open the door for her when she could have done that. Maybe she just wanted Molly as a spectator to her love affair.

It was cold and she hugged her coat so that it was tight

around her. She kept to the edge of the building and didn't strike out across the grounds until she got to the quad which had some trees and benches to give her cover. Once on the grass, she ran towards the lake, slowing down as she neared it.

Six nights before Rachel had made this very same journey.

Approaching the boathouse, Rose stopped by a tree and looked carefully at the building. She saw a haze of light coming from one of the windows. There was no sound, though. She wondered if some of the girls were trying to sleep out all night in the boathouse. She'd heard of it happening in the *summer*.

She crossed over to the wall and then moved slowly along it. When she got to the window she paused. Then, leaning forward, she looked in.

Sitting on the floor of the boathouse, surrounded by candles, was a girl who looked identical to Juliet Baker.

Rose ducked back from the window in shock.

Who was she?

She crossed her arms and hugged herself. She blew on to her hands to warm them and looked to the side. The jetty was jutting out into the lake. She couldn't see the water from where she was but she pictured it still, like glass, a thin layer of ice forming on it which would crack and disappear at the first hint of sunlight and warmth.

She leant forward again. In the flickering candlelight

Rose could see that the girl was swathed in clothes; a long coat and a shawl or throw of some sort around her shoulders. Her face was in shadow but even so there was something familiar about her.

Rose stepped back again, not wanting to be seen.

One of the girls was dressing up to look like Juliet Baker. It was the obvious explanation. But why? What was the point of such an unpleasant game?

She heard a noise; footsteps, the rustle of bushes and grasses. She backed around the corner of the boathouse as the steps grew louder. She heard a male voice swearing and, looking out, she saw Tim Baker going into the boathouse. The door closed behind him.

Juliet Baker's brother.

When she was sure he wasn't coming out again she edged along the wall and looked in the window. The girl was standing up. This time she looked different. The girl's black hair was gone. It was on the ground beside her. A wig.

Tania Miller was hugging Tim Baker. She had her arms tightly round him but his were hanging by his side. He looked angry and was speaking to her. Rose couldn't hear what they were saying but the tone was one of reproof. Tania Miller, Rachel's old friend. Dressed up to look like Tim Baker's dead sister. Tim Baker, ex-boyfriend of Rachel's, part of the deception. Rose turned away from the window, a feeling of revulsion filling her. She didn't want to waste her time looking at them.

She began to walk away when the door of the boathouse opened suddenly. She stood rigid. Whoever came out would see her there and she would be mortified, especially in front of vile Tim Baker.

But no one came out.

The voices got louder and she crept back to the window. Tim Baker was standing by the door as if he was about to leave.

'You don't love me!'

'I never said I did!'

'You made me dress up and you caused someone to die and you don't even love me!'

'I didn't make you do anything. And we didn't cause anyone to die!'

'I only did it because you said . . .'

'You knew what you were doing . . .'

There was snuffling and nose blowing.

'She was my friend . . .'

'You hadn't been friends for ages. You told me you couldn't stand her . . .'

'I didn't mean I wanted to kill her . . .'

'You didn't kill her. No one killed her. She fell in the lake. That's not our fault. Anyhow, I don't feel sorry for her. She drove my sister to her death.'

Rose tensed.

'I can't stop thinking about it . . .'

'Well, try!'

'And there's this policewoman in school. She's been speaking to Rachel's friends and I'm afraid she'll want to talk to me!'

'Why? You weren't her friend!'

'She'll arrest me!'

'You haven't committed a crime. You dressed up a bit. It was a joke. No one gets arrested for playing a joke.'

'You don't care . . .'

'Give it a rest, T. You're driving me mad.'

'I wish we hadn't done it.'

'Oh, come on, T. You loved it. You couldn't do enough of it.'

'I was an idiot. I just tried to please you and you don't even love me.'

'Grow up, T. I'm not going to tell you I love you every time we meet. I'm just not going to do it.'

There was quiet. Rose felt her mouth twist up to the side, waiting for the next exchange. Maybe they had finished arguing. Possibly Tim Baker was trying to get round Tania, trying to placate her. She didn't even want to imagine the scene.

'Tim! Don't go.'

'I'm freezing my backside off here. I'll ring you. You better get back into school. And lock the door before you go.'

Tim Baker strode out. Rose froze. He only had to look round to see her but he didn't turn back – he just cut through the trees in the direction of the drive then disappeared. From inside the boathouse Rose could hear crying. Then the faint light from the window went out and it was completely dark. Rose ducked back round the corner. She heard a shuffling sound as though Tania was moving around and then, through the dark, Tania's shape appeared at the door. She shut it and Rose heard the sound of a key being turned. With a final sob Tania took off and ran away from the boathouse. Rose made her out for a few seconds before she merged into the trees and darkness.

She was heading back to Brontë House. No doubt there was some door unlocked allowing her to go back into the building undetected. Rose walked after her, pausing to pick up something from the ground that Tania had dropped in her hurry to get away. The black wig.

Rose stood holding it for a moment.

What was it Tim Baker had said? *She drove my sister to her death.* Rose's shoulders dropped and she began to walk towards the main building. She wondered what Tim meant but really she didn't need to ask. Rachel had probably treated Juliet in the same way she'd treated Rose. The circumstances would have been different; the taunts, the hurts, the cruelties. Rachel hadn't seemed to see friendship as something to cherish. As soon as she got it she set about dismantling it, destroying it. Rose had walked away; maybe Juliet Baker hadn't been able to.

So Tim Baker and Tania decided to try and frighten Rachel.

Had it caused her death?

Had they been out here at the lake on Monday night pretending to haunt Rachel? Had she come out here looking for a ghost and found her ex-friend dressed up? On top of that Tania was with her ex-boyfriend? Was this the last straw? To find that Tim had taken up with someone else and that together they were going out of their way to try and *frighten* her?

Ten minutes later Rose was back in her room. She flung the wig on to the desk. She pulled her laptop out of her bag and opened it up. While it was loading she sat on the bed and wound the duvet around her middle, feeling the warmth come back into her hands. Then she fiddled with the pillows so that she could lean back and get comfortable.

She typed an email.

Dear Lauren Clarke, I think you should talk to Tania Miller and Tim Baker and ask them why they tried to frighten Rachel Bliss in the days/weeks before she died. Tania wore a black wig (which I have) so that at a distance she looked like Juliet Baker. I think Tania and Tim were there on the night Rachel died. That's why Rachel went out to the lake. The reason I know all this is because I overheard them talking. I'm going back to London in the morning but you can always contact me by email. Rose Smith.

She read it over a couple of times and sent it.

She placed the laptop on the floor beside the bed and rearranged the duvet so that it covered her up. She was still dressed, still wearing her boots and coat but she didn't care. She lay her head on the pillow and drifted in and out of sleep.

TWENTY-THREE

When Rose woke up properly it was 08.46 Monday morning. The girls were getting ready to start classes for the week. She must have sunk into a deep sleep because she'd slept through the wake-up call and the scramble for the showers and breakfast. She threw the duvet off. Her coat had twisted around her. She swung her feet off the bed and on to the floor and unbuttoned her coat. She got up and looked at her phone. There was no message from Joshua. Could it be that he was still asleep? Her laptop was by the side of the bed. She had one new message.

Thanks, Rose. I'm coming to the school at midday. If you could delay your departure I would like to talk to you. Lauren Clarke.

Rose huffed. Now she would have to wait around and see the police officer. *Rose, Rose, why didn't you just keep quiet about it!*

She rummaged about in her bag. She pulled out her

toiletries. She had no fresh clothes to wear but at least she could have a shower before going for breakfast. Maybe by that time Joshua would be up.

After washing she got herself some tea and toast and sat in the tiny kitchen. Joshua came in. She looked up from her tea, glad to see him. His hair was wet as though he'd not long got out of the shower. His face looked clean but there was still redness across his mouth where the tape had been.

'Morning,' he said wearily.

'You all right?' she said, reaching out her hand and touching his arm.

He nodded. 'Starving.'

'There're cereals and milk and eggs and bread here. Can you make something?'

'Sure.'

'We've got a slight problem about leaving,' she said.

He was at the cupboards getting the food out and looking for bowls. She showed him where things were and at the same time explained what had happened in the middle of the night. He looked at her with concern.

'You went out in the night after everything we'd been through at Stiffkey? Why didn't you just call one of the staff? Your old housemistress?'

She shrugged but then wondered why she hadn't. Because at heart she was still a student? And students didn't call on the staff to help in case they got another student into trouble?

Joshua was beating eggs in a bowl.

'It's a good thing that we're not rushing back to London,' he said.

'Why?'

'I'd like to go back to the cottage. To look at it in daylight.'

'Back?' Rose was nonplussed.

'We were in a state last night. I want to see if there's any other evidence that we might have missed.'

Rose had no wish to go back to that cottage now or ever.

'Rosie,' Joshua said, seeing her expression. 'The door's open. We can go inside, look around. Maybe there's something there that might help us. I want to take some shots of it. I need to send some stuff to Skeggsie so that he can get going. Start looking for links. This is the right time to do it. We can spend twenty minutes there and then get on our way.'

Rose folded her arms across her chest. She did not want to return to the cottage. But Joshua was at the hotplates, making an omelette and she was staring at his back.

'I'll go on my own if you like.'

'Oh no,' she said. 'You're not going there on your own. I'll come. But it'll be twenty minutes tops. Then I can get back in good time to see the policewoman.'

'Oh,' he said. 'Got the bracelet?'

She pulled it out of her pocket.

'Skeggsie wants a picture.'

She gave it to him and he turned back to his food.

'I'll just eat this, get packed and see you, what? Down at the car in thirty minutes?'

She mumbled something and walked off.

Back in her room she heard people moving about. It was the end of the first period and she looked out of the window and saw some students heading out of the building for different parts of the school. As the groups cleared she saw two solitary figures left. One was Molly Wallace sitting on a bench in the quad. She had her coat and hat on. She looked unhappy. Tania Miller was the other figure. She was walking across the grass and heading for Brontë House. Tania's cropped hair made her head look tiny. She wasn't wearing a coat, just a long cardigan over her uniform. She had her hands in her pockets and was looking at the ground. Rose wondered where she was going.

Rose turned away from the window and packed her stuff and for the second day running she chucked the bedclothes in the corner. She most definitely was not coming back here to sleep again. Before she left she looked at the wig sprawled on the desk where she'd thrown it the night before. She put on her coat and shoved the wig in her pocket.

Maybe Tania was ill or too upset for her classes.

Rose took her stuff downstairs and, leaving her bag in reception, she went out into the cold. Molly Wallace had gone and Rose headed for Brontë House. Once inside she paused. She didn't know Tania's room but it wasn't going to be hard to find it. The block was square with a small courtyard garden in the middle. The bedrooms were off a corridor on the ground floor. Rose walked along and looked at the name tag on each. Tania Miller's was half-way down. She knocked. There was no answer so she knocked more loudly. A grumbling sound came from inside and the door opened roughly. Tania stood there with a scowl on her face.

'What do you want?'

'You dropped something last night.'

'What?'

Rose pulled the wig out of her pocket. Tania looked at it and seemed to deflate. She turned away and slumped on to her bed. Rose walked in and closed the door behind her. She tossed the wig at Tania.

'Don't you want it? It's yours.'

'Where was it?' Tania asked cagily.

'Outside the boathouse. I picked it up after you left. Well, after you and your boyfriend left.'

Tania ran her fingers through her hair and they seemed to continue as though they had a memory of longer hair, the heavy, shiny mass that Rose had envied.

It made Rose realise something suddenly.

'He made you get your hair cut! Didn't he? So that you could get the wig on and off more easily.'

Tania picked up the wig and threw it into the corner of the room.

'You were listening to us, last night? Did you hear the way he treats me? When we first got together he was so loving, so nice and now he's different. If I'm honest, I think the only reason he paid any attention to me was so that I would go along with his little plan to upset Rachel.'

'You were her friend once.'

Tania went to speak but stopped. Then she seemed to draw a long breath.

'It was a joke at first. You know what Rachel was like. You know what how mean she was. Tim said she treated his sister badly. He's convinced that she was the cause of his sister's suicide. So he wanted to take revenge. That was all. It was meant to be a kind of joke. I waited till late at night and then I stood under the trees and shone a torch up at my face. A few times. Anybody with half a brain would have known that it was someone playing a game.'

'Molly said she believed it. Rachel wrote to me and she absolutely believed it. She also told me she saw Juliet Baker in her room once.'

'Just once. I went up there with the wig on just once. Come on, Rose, you know what she was like. She was a horrible cow.'

'That doesn't excuse what you've been doing. My God, Tania, she's dead!'

'That was nothing to do with us. Nothing. The last time we did it was Friday night. Three nights before she died. That was it. We stopped.'

'So you weren't dressed up like a ghost on Monday when she died.'

'No, but . . .'

'What?'

'We were in the boathouse and she caught us there. We weren't *doing* anything. We were drinking vodka and Tim was smoking dope. She just barged in. She went mad at Tim. She kept saying, *How could you bring her here?* So I guess Tim and she must have spent time there as well. He just laughed at her. It was like this was what he'd waited for. He just told her to get lost and then she picked up the bottle of vodka and said she was taking it to Mrs Abbott and we would both be in a lot of trouble. Then she stormed off. Tim was furious. He went back to his car and he told me to race back to my room before Rachel told anyone. Then it was her word against ours. So I locked up and ran back to Brontë. I didn't see her. The next thing I heard on Tuesday morning was that she was in the lake . . .'

Tania's voice was cracking.

'That was nothing to do with us. As far as we were concerned Rachel went off to the main building to wake up Mrs Abbott. She took our vodka with her. I expected Mrs Abbott to come to my room for the rest of the night and when she didn't I just thought Rachel had got cold feet. She was no angel and she only knew about the boathouse because she'd been there with him weeks before.'

'Why didn't you tell the police about this?'

'Oh, Miss Rose Goody Two-Shoes. I'm really going to go and own up to seeing a guy in the boathouse in the middle of the night. Can you imagine my mum's face?'

Rose looked at Tania with distaste. Rachel was dead and all she could think of was being in trouble with her mum.

'Well,' Rose said, picking up the wig from the floor of Tania's room, 'I expect your mum won't look too pleased when she hears that you were dressing up as a dead girl and standing in the grounds late at night in order to frighten someone out of their wits.'

'How?'

'I told the policewoman about finding you last night. I'm guessing she'll be speaking to you sometime today.'

Rose walked out of Tania's room.

Moments later she heard Tania's door slam loudly behind her.

She left Brontë house and saw Molly Wallace hanging around the entrance.

'Hi, Molly,' she said.

Beyond Molly she saw Joshua waiting by Skeggsie's Mini.

'Rose, you know we talked about the ghost?'

'Actually, I don't have time to chat now, Molly. I'm on my way out. I'll be back in an hour or so.'

Molly put her hand on Rose's sleeve. 'Everything I said was true. Rachel *was* really upset by it but on Sunday evening she came to my room and she was in a real state. She'd just been walking past Brontë House and she said she got a terrible shock. She looked in Tania's room and saw her standing in front of the mirror wearing a wig and looking just like Juliet. She knew then what had happened. She knew that someone had been messing around with her.'

Joshua was waving at Rose. Rose gave a distracted wave back.

'She knew Tania was dressing up as Juliet?'

Molly nodded.

'Did you tell the police this?'

'No.'

'Molly!' Rose said, exasperated. 'These details are important. Look, the policewoman is coming here at twelve. Make sure you see her. Tell her what you've just told me.'

'I was just keeping a confidence. Rachel told me not to tell anyone. She said she felt enough of a fool.'

'Rachel is dead, Molly,' she said tersely. 'Speak to the policewoman when she comes. Look, I've got to go.'

She walked off towards Joshua. Halfway across the grass she paused. Had she been too harsh on Molly? She turned around but there was no sign of her. She had gone.

Rose walked on, quickening her step to get to the car.

TWENTY-FOUR

In the car she told Joshua about her visit to Tania. He asked a couple of questions but she sensed that his heart really wasn't in it. He was thinking of the visit to the cottage. He reversed the car quickly and made his way up the drive to the lane in silence. She looked at his profile. His face was tense and there was a slight frown on his forehead. The previous night had been awful, worse for him but still he was determined to continue what he had started. His visit to the Kensington restaurant had stirred a nest of vipers but he didn't care – he wanted to continue his search.

How different she was. She just wanted to go home and try and forget about it all. No matter that it was all some-how linked to her mother and Brendan.

And yet she had just gone to see Tania when there was no need. She'd given the information to WPC Lauren Clarke who would no doubt see Tania when she came to the school later that day. Why had Rose done that? To see for herself what Tania had to say? To get a sense of whether Tania was sorry? She pulled at the edge of her pink socks, making sure they were straight. Maybe she wasn't so different to Joshua after all.

They drove through Stiffkey and Rose glanced at the cottages and the White Rose as they passed. They turned along the beach road and parked in the small car park, deserted just as it had been both times before. Joshua pulled on the handbrake which made a doleful creak.

'Do we have to do this?' she said. 'Why not go to the police? What happened here, that's real. We have the name of this Russian. We could identify the man who tied you up. It might be possible to find out something through official channels.'

Joshua was shaking his head.

'Rosie,' he said softly, taking her hand in his, 'I have to do this. Lev mentioned my dad's name. He threatened him. His father is the key to this. I can't stop now and hand it all over to the police. They'll just fold it up into their files and notes and we'll never hear another word about it.'

Rose didn't answer. Joshua was rubbing her hand distractedly. She sat very still, feeling his fingers making circles on her skin. It sent ripples up her arm and across her chest. She thought of the previous evening, in the car, when she'd wanted to kiss him.

'How is your mouth?' she said.

He picked her hand up and carried it across to his face. He ran her fingers across his skin.

'It feels a bit better,' he said.

Her throat felt dry. His skin was prickly and rough, his face warm. She stared outside at the mudflats which were perfectly still and wondered whether something was happening between them.

'We should go,' she whispered.

Moments later he opened the door, letting an icy blast into the car. Rose got out and hugged herself. The morning air was crisp and clung to her skin. She'd left her gloves behind again. She pulled her cuffs down over her wrists and started to walk.

Joshua asked her more about Rachel Bliss as they walked towards the path. Rose answered while looking at the vastness of the sky, and the flocks of birds swirling about, dipping and diving, floating on the air currents. At one point she stopped still, leaning backwards to see a tiny plane miles above, leaving a vapour trail. Joshua saw her.

'Bombers. Lots of RAF missions fly round here.'

There was no one else to be seen. The mudflats stretched away into the distance. She thought of the night before, the sound of the car coming at her from far away, the eerie rumble of its engine as it crept along under cover of darkness.

'Skeggsie's feeling better,' Joshua said. 'I Skyped him

this morning. He looks a bit rough but he's keen to get on. He told me that he's got an idea about the code of *The Butterfly Project*. He might have something to show us this afternoon.'

Codes, spies and the Russian secret service. Rose was beginning to feel as though she'd gone back in time to some James Bond film when people had codewords and knives that flicked out of the front of their shoes. A bit of her wanted to laugh, to make fun of it all, but she sensed that Joshua wouldn't like that. He was serious; never more. She'd just have to bide her time and hope that the whole national security thing fizzled out. Maybe there was some other explanation for Lev Baranski following Joshua to Norfolk.

'We'll do the house first, then the boathouse . . .' Joshua said. 'I'll take a lot of pictures.'

They turned off the path and headed down the lane towards the cottage. Looking down, Rose noticed the fresh tyre tracks of the SUV. There were several ruts and she wondered exactly how many times it had gone back and forth to the cottage. Then something awful occurred to her.

'You don't think Lev Baranski is back at the cottage now? Some of these tyre tracks look brand new.'

'No, he's had his say. He's given me his message. If he wanted to do any more he would have done it last night.'

'Still, I don't remember this many.'

'It was dark.'

She nodded. She probably hadn't been looking at the ground at all, just feeling the unevenness under her feet. Up ahead she could see a flash of white. The cottage was coming into sight and seconds later she was relieved to see that there was no SUV parked in front of it. It looked just the way it had the day before. Deserted.

Joshua quickened his pace. He went ahead and then stopped suddenly as if halted by an invisible wall.

'What's up?' she said.

'I don't know. It feels funny, different.'

'How do you mean?'

Rose stood beside him and looked around. The cottage seemed just the same, the door at an angle where it had been opened forcefully the previous afternoon. Rose looked at the land behind. It was quiet, a bird tweeting melodically from some distant tree.

And yet there was something different.

She looked down at the ground. The rutted path had been smoothed out; it was flatter than she remembered. Joshua walked away while she focused on the ground in front of the cottage, as if someone had patted it down, like sand that had been levelled.

'Look.'

She walked on, following Joshua into the cottage.

He was standing in the middle of the living room.

It was empty. There was not a stick of furniture left.

'Oh, my,' she said.

'Someone's cleared it out.'

They both stared in disbelief.

At the back of the cottage was the window where she had worked at poking a hole in the wood. Now the wood was gone and there was just a space, the broken glass letting the cold wind in. She went closer and saw that the planks had been ripped off and thrown into what had once been the back garden.

'Who's done this?'

'Baranski?'

Joshua shook his head.

'This must have been done last night or this morning. I don't get it,' Rose said.

'The boat?' Joshua said.

He strode off in the direction of the outbuilding. Rose went after him, across the smoothed forecourt and followed him into the dark interior. She stopped still, looking at an empty space.

The boat was gone.

The building was bare, as if there had never been a boat there. The boat, the struts it had sat on, the tarpaulin that had covered it, they had all vanished. She walked across to the space where it had been moored, to the wall that she had sat up against, the corner in which she had scrabbled about and found the identity bracelet. There was no sign of it, no scrapes, no crumbling wood, no dust. There wasn't even the strong smell of brine that had clung to her nostrils the night before.

'Someone's been here and stripped the place. They must have done this in the night or early this morning. Who?'

Rose thought of the night before, of the text she had sent on her mobile.

'I contacted Frank Richards.'

'What?'

'I called the number he gave me. It went out of my head when everything else happened. I was in a panic and I only had a bit of charge on my phone and I didn't know who to call.'

'You spoke to him?'

'I sent a text.'

'What did you say?'

She pulled her phone out of her pocket and looked up the last text she had sent. **I'm in trouble. Baranski has Josh in the Stiffkey Cottage. Help me.**

'I tried to send it but there was no signal so I forgot about it and it was only after they left and we were heading back to the car that the message went. I just thought, *Oh, too late to be of any use.*'

Joshua had Rose's phone in his hand and he started to walk back and forth, a spring in his step.

'Don't you see?' he said, his voice high with excitement. 'This means that this place *is* important. So important that someone, not just one person, some *team* have been here to clean it up, to strip it. They know we've been here. They know through that phone number, through Frank Richards. This isn't just Dad and Kathy and Frank Richards. This is more than that. It must be to do with national security. No other organisation would have such immediate resources to clean this place. We are close to something, Rose.'

Rose felt trepidation. Something important had happened. She held out her hand for her phone and read over her message. At first it was her mother and Brendan who disappeared. Then Frank Richards was linked to it. Then the Russians. Now she pictured men in dark clothes, vans, lorries, a boat trailer, all marching across the mudflats in the middle of the night to clear the cottage in case two teenagers came back to find out some more about it. They'd even smoothed out the ground in front of the cottage to cover up their tracks.

They'd taken the boat that was called *Butterfly* before she and Joshua had had a chance to look inside it. Rose left the outbuilding and stood in front of the cottage. She looked around and then up into the air. Someone somewhere had known that they were there and had swooped in and snatched any evidence that might have been there for them.

Joshua was right. Something was happening that was bigger than her mother and Brendan.

A beep sounded. Joshua got his mobile out. It was a text.

'Skeggsie,' he said and read it.

'What?' she said, seeing a wide smile on his face.

'You won't believe this. The name on the identity bracelet. The unpronounceable Russian word. In English it's *Viktor*.'

Viktor Baranski, whose dead body was found just off the pier at Cromer.

'What are we going to do?' she said.

'We're going to find Dad and Kathy.'

She nodded. She really believed that they would.

TWENTY-FIVE

'I just have to see the policewoman,' Rose said, leaving Joshua in the reception area. 'Then I'll get my stuff and we'll be off.'

Joshua nodded but he'd already opened his laptop.

'I'll stay here. Email these photos to Skeggsie.'

Rose smiled. She walked away feeling brighter than she had for days. It wouldn't be long until they got under way to London. Once back there they could continue with their search. Skeggsie had said he might have a solution to some of the code in *The Butterfly Project*. For the first time she felt really interested in the dusty old book and Frank Richards' notebooks. And Joshua was right. Something was going on that was bigger than her mother and Brendan. They were a part of something. Could it be to do with national security? Had her mother and Brendan stumbled on something to do with the death of Viktor Baranski which had made them go on the run?

She headed for Mrs Abbott's rooms. It was as if she was

a student again, used to going back and forth, the school a kind of second family home for her. She thought of Anna who was due back in Belsize Park later that day. She wondered if, after their respective weekends away, they might have a coffee in the kitchen. She felt better and better about this because, if they really were on the way to finding out the truth, then Anna would regret the comments she made about Brendan.

Maybe things would take a turn for the better.

Coming up to Mrs Abbott's room she felt her mood falter. Rachel Bliss's suicide had still happened. A girl's life was over.

WPC Lauren Clarke was in Mrs Abbott's conference room again.

'Rose, thank you for waiting to see me,' she said briskly, as if she too was in a hurry. 'I must say you seem to have an ability to find things out. Have you ever thought of joining the police?'

'No.'

'You should. There are a number of good graduate courses . . .'

Rose pulled the black wig out of her pocket and laid it on the table. Lauren Clarke fished out a plastic bag and placed the wig inside it.

'Thank you.'

'I've spoken to Tania Miller. She said it was Tim Baker's idea to try and frighten Rachel . . .'

'I thought I was asking the questions?' Lauren Clarke said, a thin smile on her face.

'I was here. I saw her out of class on her own. It was too good an opportunity to miss. She also told me that she and Tim were up at the boathouse on Monday night when Rachel found them together . . .'

Lauren Clarke looked irritated but Rose carried on.

'Tim Baker had a key from when his father worked here and they used the boathouse. Apparently when Rachel was his girlfriend they went there as well.'

'Thank you, Rose. We'll be able to ascertain those details when *we* continue with *our* enquiries.'

Rose tutted out loud. The policewoman's words irritated her. She was reminded of the times she had heard similar phrases: *We are following up our enquiries. Enquiries are taking place. Our enquiries are ongoing.*

'You have an attitude, Rose, if you don't mind me saying.'

'If I do it's because I've spoken to police officers like yourself many times. Whenever I asked them about my mother I never got a straight answer. And I don't know what's worse,' Rose said, her thoughts coming straight out, as if this woman represented every police officer she'd ever spoken to. 'Whether they're just covering up what they do know – in other words, lying – or whether they genuinely haven't got a clue.'

Lauren Clarke was looking at her with concern now.

'I spoke to Tania Miller because I didn't want to wait and ask you what she'd said and be fobbed off with, *We are following up our enquiries.*'

'I see. Is that what happened on Saturday? Did I fob you off then?'

'No, but I had to work hard to get some answers.'

'OK, let's stop this. You have done me a service even though we frown on members of the public doing things for themselves but I appreciate that as soon as you got your information you passed it straight on to me. Now I will share some information with you on the basis that it is confidential.'

'Of course,' Rose said, as nicely as she could.

'And as a point of fact Tim Baker told me that he and his girlfriend were in the boathouse when Rachel found them. This you already know. The new information is that Tim Baker has a very particular reason for not liking Rachel. He blames his sister's suicide on her.'

'I know . . .'

Lauren Clarke put one finger in the air to silence Rose.

'It appears that Tim Baker was helping to clear out his sister's room in the summer and he found a notebook, a kind of ad hoc diary that Juliet had kept. She had written down things that Rachel Bliss had said about her father who had lost his job at the school. He was gardener here for seven months, then he was made redundant. Apparently Rachel had suggested to Juliet that her father had been dismissed because he'd touched one of the girls inappropriately. Sexual misconduct. It's not true, of course. I checked with Mrs Abbott. But Juliet believed it.'

Rose blew through her teeth. What had been wrong with Rachel Bliss? Why had she told so many lies? Possibly it had been to put her at the centre of any drama; make it seem as though she knew everything there was to know. And it wouldn't have mattered a jot if it hadn't always been at the cost of other people.

'The second thing I've learned is from the autopsy report. It's been confirmed that Rachel did have high levels of alcohol in her blood. I mentioned this to you the other day. It's also been confirmed – and this bit I didn't tell you – that Rachel had a head injury.'

'Oh? Someone hit her?'

Rose was startled by this information. All the times that she had thought about this she had never considered the possibility that someone had deliberately *killed* Rachel.

'Not necessarily. A blow to the head could have been caused by a weapon or an accident. She was found near the jetty. Let's suppose that she did, in fact, fall off the jetty. She could have hit her head on the edge of the walkway and then went into the water. Or someone could have hit her with an object. A bottle perhaps. It appears from the autopsy that it wasn't the blow that killed her. She certainly drowned but the injury may have meant that, along with the alcohol, she was in no fit state to swim or catch hold of the steps up to the jetty and help herself in any way.'

'Maybe Tim Baker . . . Maybe after Tania went back to school he hung around and found Rachel with the vodka. Maybe he took the bottle from her and hit her with it.'

Rose found herself stirred up. It made sense. It was also an appealing idea that the vile Tim Baker might have been responsible for Rachel's death.

'He denies it. He told me about seeing Rachel on Monday night as soon as I saw him. He gave me a full account and insists that once she left the boathouse he went off to his car and he never set eyes on her again.'

'He hated Rachel!'

'I know. I'll be interviewing him again and Tania and, who knows, maybe their explanation might change. And don't forget – when all is said and done it could have been just an accident.'

Rose sat back. She felt tired; the previous night was weighing on her. The euphoria she had felt at the cottage and on the drive back to school had faded.

'But thank you for your help. Your intervention made a number of things clearer which was why I suggested that you should think of a career in the police. Your mother thought it a good profession.'

'It was because my mother was in the police that I lost her. And my stepdad.'

'Brendan Johnson.'

Rose nodded.

'Did you know, by the way, that Rachel Bliss had done a lot of research about your mother and her partner? There are files full of stuff about it on her laptop.'

Rose nodded. 'When we were first friends she was fascinated by it.'

'Yes, she did some then, but she also spent a lot of time six months ago revisiting the case. As if she'd had a renewed interest. I wonder why that was?'

Rose didn't answer. She remembered Rachel coming up to her in the quad after an exam and announcing that she'd seen Rose's mother on the pier at Cromer. Even now it gave her a soft ache in her chest. Rachel using every lie that she could to draw Rose in. Now all that was left of Rachel was her virtual footsteps, wandering from website to website. She would tell no more lies to anyone.

'Her research filled me in on the details of the case.'

'Wasn't it on police files?'

'I looked on Saturday after we spoke but the information is classified. They must have been important people, Rose. If files are classified it means that they have had the highest attention so you needn't worry that your mother and stepfather have been forgotten about.'

Classified files. Hidden away. Only for certain people's eyes.

'Anyway, I'll let you get on your way. Do have a safe journey to London.'

Rose stood up. 'Thanks. Sorry if I was a bit . . .'

'Of a pain?'

'Thanks, anyway.'

'My pleasure. Look after yourself, Rose.'

Mrs Abbott was waiting outside. The head teacher had an anxious look on her face. She ushered Rose into her office.

'I heard you stayed an extra night, Rose. I hope your friend has recovered from his fall?'

Rose had to think for a moment. Then she remembered the story she had told Martha Harewood.

'Yes, yes. I appreciate you allowing me to stay. And my friend.'

'I have something for you. Mr and Mrs Bliss passed it on to me. They found it among Rachel's things.'

Mrs Abbott held out a large padded envelope. Rose took it. On the front was her name and her address in Belsize Park. It was in Rachel's handwriting. There were several stamps on it.

'I imagine that Rachel intended to post it to you. She didn't but it is addressed to you and Mr and Mrs Bliss especially wanted you to have it.'

'Thank you.'

'You're off back to London now?'

'Yes. Thanks again for letting me stay.'

'It's been a terrible time. You must come back some time for a visit when things are calm. You know, Rose, you were an unhappy girl when you arrived here. With good reason, of course. I do hope we were able to help you in some small way.'

Rose suddenly felt tearful. Of course they had helped. They had been a sort of family for her when she had none. They had given her warmth and affection and support when she needed it most. She wanted to say this to Mrs Abbott but didn't trust herself to speak. Instead she nodded tightly, embarrassed at her emotions.

'Good! Take care on the roads, especially as it gets dark.'

Closing the door to Mrs Abbott's room, she tucked the envelope under her arm and headed to find Joshua at the reception area.

TWENTY-SIX

Rose and Joshua carried their bags out to the car. It was almost two o'clock. The day had disappeared and they still had the long drive ahead of them. As they were packing their things in the back, Rose saw Amanda heading towards her.

'Are you off?' Amanda said.

'Yes.'

'I just saw Tania. She says that the police have interviewed Tim Baker. She says that someone hit Rachel on the head with a bottle and that the police were asking Tim about it!'

'I did hear something about it but it's not certain. It could have been an accident,' Rose said weakly, not wanting to give too much away. 'However, it appears Tim Baker is not a nice person. No doubt he'll finish with Tania, then he'll be looking for someone new. Make sure it's no one you know.'

A couple of other girls were heading in their direction. They called out to Rose and Amanda.

'You coming, Rose?' Joshua said politely.

'You could introduce me, Rose.'

Amanda looked at Joshua with open admiration. Rose flinched.

'This is my . . . my friend Josh.'

Amanda said. 'Are you at uni?'

Joshua nodded. 'Engineering, Queen Mary College.'

'I might apply for London University. I hear the night-life is very good there.'

Rose interrupted. 'Where's Molly? I was a bit short with her before.'

'I haven't seen her all day. She wasn't in French or History. Good news is her mother's picking her up today.'

The other girls reached them. It was Moira and Sandy, two girls who Rose had spent a bit of time with. They both had silly looks on their faces, glancing back and forth at Joshua.

'Have you seen Molly?' Amanda said to them.

'I saw her about half an hour ago, just after lunch. She was heading off to the lake. Not sure why she's going there unless it's the Rachel thing again.'

The Rachel thing. Is that how it will end up? Rose wondered. Those words, *the Rachel thing*, would cover the events of the last week. A young girl's body being dragged out of the water of the school lake. A pale corpse lying on the jetty while the groundsman and gardener tried to resuscitate her. An unhappy girl who spread her misery among other people. Now she was gone and it would all be remembered as *the Rachel thing*.

'Shall we make a move?' Joshua called.

'See you, girls.'

Each of them stepped forward to give Rose a kiss. Embarrassed by their show of friendliness, Rose held her cheek out.

'Remember what I said about Tim Baker,' she shouted, getting into the car and pulling on her seat belt.

Joshua reversed and then they moved away from the school building and went slowly along the winding drive-way, going over speed humps, pausing to let some students pass in front of them. A few metres on Rose looked round and the girls had gone. She turned back and saw, over to her left, the lake and the boathouse. Molly had gone there, one of the girls said. She remembered how brusque she had been with her. It made her feel awful. Molly had been the only person who seemed to care about Rachel's death. Molly, who had lost a friend. Why on earth hadn't Rose been a bit softer with her, given her a few extra minutes of her time?

'Joshua?'

'Yes?'

'Do you mind if we turn left at the next lane and just head down to the boathouse. There's someone I want to say goodbye to?'

'Another hold-up!'

'Come on. I went back to the cottage with you. This'll be ten minutes. No more. The girl I want to speak to might not even be there but at least I will have tried.'

The lane was coming up and Rose smiled when she saw Joshua indicate.

'Thanks,' she said.

Molly was at the end of jetty. Rose saw her as soon as she turned the corner of the boathouse. She was sitting down, her back against the wall, staring out at the lake. Rose waved at her and smiled but Molly didn't respond. For a moment Rose wondered if Molly hadn't seen her or whether she was upset because Rose had been sharp with her earlier on.

She looked back at Joshua sitting in the front seat of the car. He'd parked alongside one of the Mary Linton School minibuses. He was talking on his mobile. No doubt another conversation with Skeggsie about what had happened and what they were going to do.

She walked round the boathouse and on to the jetty. The lake was still and cold with a thin mist forming above the surface. Her feet sounded on the wood and she kept a smile on her face, hoping that Molly would cheer up when she got closer.

'Hi,' Rose said, when she reached her.

'Oh, hi,' Molly said as if she'd only just noticed Rose was there.

Molly's hair was pulled back in a tie and she was wearing a dark jacket over her uniform. She had thick tights on and knee-length boots. For once she had no silly slides in her hair.

'Having a break out here?' Rose said, looking down on her.

Molly nodded.

'Get away from everyone talking about Rachel?'

She nodded again.

Rose felt awkward standing up. She pulled her jacket down so that it comfortably covered her bottom and then sat down on the planks, crossing her legs and leaning back against the wall. She felt the cold immediately and wondered how long Molly had been sitting there.

'Look, Molly, I was a bit rude earlier when you were telling me about Rachel seeing Tania dressed up . . .'

Rose realised then that she hadn't told Lauren Clarke that piece of information. In the face of all the new things she'd heard it had been completely forgotten. Maybe it was of little importance.

'It's all right, Rose, I know you didn't mean it.'

'I think the police are beginning to piece together what happened. They know that Rachel came out here late on Monday night and found Tim and Tania together in the boathouse. There was a row and Rachel stormed off with their bottle of vodka. She threatened to tell Mrs Abbott but then I think she must have just come down here and sat drinking the vodka by herself.'

Molly nodded.

'So it'll all be over soon,' Rose said, using a soft voice and patting Molly on the arm.

'I'm not a child, Rose – don't treat me like one,' Molly said, pulling her arm away.

'I wasn't . . .'

'Everyone treats me as though I'm a child. I'm not. I've got brains. I've got feelings. That's why I liked being friends with Rachel. She didn't treat me like a child.'

'She was difficult, though.'

'I knew all that. I knew what she was like. I'd seen her over the years. When *we* got together she seemed different. We used to spend a lot of time in her room and we'd talk and she asked me all about my life and then she'd tell me about hers.'

Rose wondered if Rachel told Molly the truth or simply fabricated another life, new parents, new siblings, new problems. She shivered with the cold. Now wasn't the time to puncture Molly's memories of her dead friend.

'Aren't you cold?'

Molly shook her head. 'I helped Rachel. I was a good friend to her.'

'I know.'

'When she needed someone she knew she could trust me. When she was seeing Tim Baker and slipping out in the night she knew she could depend on me to let her back into the school. I keep my phone by my pillow and when she sent a text I went downstairs and opened the door and let her in. She never got caught and that was because of me.'

Rose remembered going out of the laundry door very early that morning. She'd left the door on the snib to stop it shutting.

'But the last few weeks she'd been different. Unhappy. She said she was being haunted and it made her snappy and horrible. I felt sorry for her. I tried to talk her out of it. I didn't for one minute think it was a ghost but she did. That's why she was so furious when she saw Tania dressed up to look like Juliet Baker. She came to my room. That was the first time ever! She came to my room and she went mad.'

Rose instinctively went to pat Molly's arm but held back. Molly was fired up, talking non-stop. Rose's eyes drifted in the direction of the boathouse and car park behind it. Was Joshua getting impatient? He would have to wait.

'She stayed in my room all evening and it was like she was the Rachel who had first been friends with me. But the next day she got angry again. She kept telling me to go away. She said some cruel things to me. *You're just a kid. Grow up. Leave me alone. Stop following me around.* She said I was like a puppy dog.'

Rose felt a flash of guilt. She had been part of this once.

'She didn't answer my texts and I didn't see her around. So I just went to my room after dinner. I went to bed and about midnight I got this text. Look, I've kept it.'

Molly got her phone out of her coat pocket. She fiddled with it. Rose rubbed her freezing hands together. Molly passed her mobile over. Rose read the text from Rachel.

Just seen Tania going out with torch. Trying the ghost bit again??? Going to follow her. I'll text when I need the door unlocked.

'Even though she hadn't bothered with me all day she still wanted me to open the door for her.'

Molly had misery written all over her face.

'Molly, my friend's in his car over there. Why don't you get in and we'll take you back to Eliot House. Your mother might have arrived.'

'I don't want to!'

'Look,' Rose found herself getting irritated, 'Rachel Bliss was a real hard case. I can't begin to tell you how she messed around with me when we were friends. How she . . . how she broke me up, lied to me, hurt my feelings. She wasn't a true friend to me ever and the truth is she wouldn't have made anyone a good friend.'

Rose could see Molly's eyes filling with tears.

'But to die in the water?'

'It's horrible,' Rose said. 'But it doesn't excuse the way she treated you, or me. Or Juliet Baker. And maybe it was an accident or maybe she drove Tim Baker mad and he just flipped out at her . . .'

Molly shook her head. 'No, Tim Baker wasn't even here.'

'What?'

'Tim Baker wasn't around. When I got here Rachel was on her own.'

'You were *here*? On Monday night?'

'I was waiting for her text. To open the door. When it got to one o'clock and she hadn't contacted me I was worried. So I got dressed and came out. I had to wedge the door open with a box. I was in a state. I was sure someone would walk past the laundry and we would get caught. I headed in the direction of the boathouse. It was dark when I got there and I didn't know what had happened. So I walked on to the jetty and there she was sitting down. Drinking straight from a bottle.'

Rose held her breath.

'She got up when she saw me. She came towards me. She was staggering all over the place. Drunk. I could smell the alcohol on her. It was bitterly cold and she had her coat hanging open. I grabbed her hand and said she should come back and sleep it off. She started talking about Tim and Tania and calling Tania horrible names. I tried to calm her but she was riled up and then she turned on me. She said, *What are you doing here? Leave me alone. I'm sick of the sight of you.* She was stumbling all over the place. I said, *Be careful, you'll fall in* and she just laughed at me. *Go back in, little girl*, she said.'

Rose listened in total silence. A terrible feeling was taking hold of her. She wanted to put her hands over her ears so that she couldn't hear any more.

'She came staggering towards me and thrust the bottle at me. *Have a drink*, she said. *Oh no, I forgot you're just a little girl. You can't drink . . .*'

Rose grabbed Molly's hand firmly, ready to overcome her resistance if she needed to. But Molly's hand was soft and floppy and cold.

'I pushed her. She fell back and lost her footing and the next thing I heard was the splash of the water and she was gone.'

'Oh, Molly.'

'I got down the steps, I called out. I expected to see her splashing about but there wasn't a sound. It was all black and there was no movement, nothing.'

'Why didn't you call someone?'

'I just ran back to school and went up to my room. I thought that somehow she might have got out. You know, been quiet to frighten me and that once I'd gone she'd swum to the side and got out and I half expected to see her the next morning.'

Rose could see Joshua at the beginning of the jetty. She pulled Molly up to a standing position.

'Come and sit in the car. I'll call Lauren Clarke, the policewoman. You need to tell her all about this. You do know that, don't you, Molly?'

'I'm not a child. I do know what I have to do.'

Rose took Molly's arm and they began to walk towards the boathouse.

TWENTY-SEVEN

The drive back to London started almost an hour later than they planned. The early part of the journey saw Rose staring out of the window, the road whooshing past. It was bright but trying to rain, spots hitting at the glass, making it glisten for a moment before fading under the late afternoon sun. It looked cold. They passed people who were pulling their coats tight. Inside the car it felt hot. Rose had already taken her coat off.

After Lauren Clarke had come to the boathouse car park and taken Molly Wallace away, Rose and Joshua had sat in the car while she explained. He'd been surprised. He'd asked several questions but none of them were easy to answer because he hadn't known Molly the way she had and he hadn't known Rachel. A weariness came over her and she said she didn't want to talk about it any more. She just wanted to get back to London.

So they'd set off through the country lanes and then on to the main road. Joshua kept a steady pace and it wasn't long before there were signs for Swaffham. The traffic slowed and Rose saw different school uniforms as parents and children mingled on the pavements. Teenagers stood around in groups and she saw their mouths opening and shutting; a day's gossip coming out, one story after another about this lesson and that friendship. Then they would disappear on to the bus and head home.

At Mary Linton most people didn't head home. The joys and sadnesses of the day were carried over into the evening. Juliet Baker *had* taken her troubles home with her. Why had she never told her family about what Rachel had said about her father? She'd kept it hidden inside herself until it had turned against her; a piece of spiteful shrapnel lodged there by Rachel to cause maximum damage later. Molly too had been isolated and her hurt feelings had grown until they exploded on the jetty that evening and Rachel got pushed into the lake.

Molly had said that there was silence when she went into the water. Had Rachel hit her head on the jetty and gone into the lake unconscious? Was that why she had sunk without a struggle? An inert object that plummeted to the bottom of the lake and floated back to the surface later to be found by the groundsman when daylight broke. She closed her eyes. She felt heavy with tiredness or sadness or both. Rachel Bliss, a damaged, *dangerous* girl who had smashed her way into people's lives. Molly Wallace, a lonely girl who people largely ignored because of her supposed immaturity. Molly's life would never be the same.

What a mess.

Once out of the town the country road was like a pale ribbon weaving through the fields. It headed off into the dusk and Rose's eyes sought out the failing light. Soon it would be dark. She'd done this drive a number of times with Anna but Anna's car was bigger and she'd been higher up. Skeggsie's Mini was low to the ground and every time another car passed them she felt like she was rumbling along the tarmac. She hadn't noticed this discomfort on the journey to the school three days before. How long ago that seemed.

Joshua put on some music and as it played she felt him reach across and squeeze her hand. She looked at his profile and wondered about the closeness they had had over the last few days. Had it just been the affection of a surrogate brother? Or had something else been happening? Could it be that his feelings for her were changing? Or was she reading too much into it? Projecting the desire she felt on to him, because that's how she wanted it to be.

She didn't know and wasn't going to ask.

As it grew dark the rain started properly. It seemed to throw itself against the windscreen and blurred the view for a split second before the wiper cleared it. Other cars came towards them with a halo of light that dazzled for a moment, then lessened as they passed. Rose closed her eyes. She could hear the music, the straining of the engine and the splash of water as they drove through wet roads.

In Brandon she sat up when the car stopped at a level crossing. A train thundered past; just one carriage, lit up like a fairground ride. They went through the town stopping and starting, the evening traffic heavy. She glanced over at Joshua, who looked tired.

'You OK driving?'

Rose turned to grab some water from her bag on the back seat of the car. She noticed the padded envelope and picked it up.

'I'm fine,' Joshua said, glancing at her. 'What's that?'

The envelope looked old, the corners of it crumpled up as though it had been sitting somewhere for a while.

'Mrs Abbott gave it to me. Rachel's parents had it apparently. They found it among Rachel's things. It should have been posted to me but never was.'

'You opened it?'

'No. Not just yet,' she said. 'Maybe when I get back home.'

She replaced it on the back seat.

'You feeling any better?'

'A bit. The further we get away from the school the better I'll feel.'

'Another hour or so. Then we'll be back in London.'

They continued along pitch-dark country lanes. After a while they joined a dual carriageway where the traffic was heavier and then on to the motorway heading for London. The rain was spearing down and spray rose up at them from passing vehicles. Rose stretched her arms out, moving her head from side to side to stop getting stiff.

'Not long now,' Joshua said. 'When's your gran getting back?'

Rose found herself smiling at Joshua's use of the word *gran*. It conjured up a completely different person from Anna. Someone tactile, easy, someone who made people laugh and who called their grandchild by a loving nickname; *Honey* or *Sweetie or Love* or even just *Rosie*, like Joshua did.

'She's coming back this evening. I guess I'll see her then. Can I come back to yours for a while?'

'Sure. Let's get a takeaway. We've got a lot to talk to Skeggsie about. Are you sure you want to do this tonight? After everything that's happened?'

'I need to do this tonight. I need to get all this other stuff out of my head.'

'Good.'

Joshua was looking for somewhere to park. After a while they found a spot a short walk away from the flat and they got out, picking up their bags. They walked along crowded pavements, falling into single file as they turned on to Camden High Street and headed for Lettuce and Stuff and the door to the flat.

'We'll get settled in and then I'll go for a takeaway.'

Rose nodded, standing in front of Joshua's front door, looking forward to seeing Skeggsie with his heavy black-rimmed glasses and buttoned-up clothes and room full of computers. They had information to swap and things to do. After being mired in the details of Rachel's last hours Rose was pleased to be away, submerged in the noise and crowds of Camden, and keen to get more involved in The Notebook project. The door to the flat opened. Rose was expecting to hear the bolts pulled back but then she remembered that Skeggsie had stopped locking himself in.

He stood there in front of them. He had an odd expression on his face.

'What's up, Skeggs?' Joshua said, pushing past him, making his way up the stairs two at a time.

'Hi, Skeggsie,' Rose said, stepping into the hallway.

Joshua was already at the top.

'You've got a visitor,' Skeggsie said. 'But don't worry. All the notebooks stuff is under lock and key.'

'Visitor?'

Rose started to walk up the stairs. She could hear Joshua's voice from above. When she got to the top she saw a man standing in the middle of the hallway. He was wearing a Crombie coat. He looked familiar and yet she couldn't place him.

'Rose Smith. It's been a long time. Five years I think.'

She narrowed her eyes. Her hip was still feeling sore from the roughing up they had had on Sunday evening.

And she was stiff after sitting so long in the car. She knew this man. There was something about him. Then it came to her.

'Chief Inspector Munroe.'

He smiled. 'Ex-Chief Inspector. I left the force a couple of years ago. I'm a civil servant now. Hence the city clothes.'

He had a jolly expression on his face as if he was a double-glazing salesman. She remembered him sitting across the coffee table in Anna's drawing room, telling her that the police would not stop searching for the truth, that they would find out what had happened to her mother and Brendan. She turned to Joshua. He looked confused. He didn't know Chief inspector Munroe.

'What do you want?' Joshua said abruptly.

'Is there somewhere we can sit and talk? Your flatmate has kept me standing in the hallway for the last ten minutes.'

Joshua pushed open the kitchen door. James Munroe walked in ahead of them. He unbuttoned the Crombie but didn't take it off. He sat down, his coat dipping on to the floor.

'What do you want?' Joshua said.

Skeggsie was standing in the doorway. James Munroe turned to look at him.

'This is a confidential matter.'

'He stays,' Joshua said. 'He's family.'

'Right.'

Skeggsie moved into the room and pulled out a chair and sat on it. James Munroe ignored him, looking at Joshua and then Rose and then back to Joshua.

'I understand that you've just come from Norfolk. In particular from Stiffkey and while there you were at the cottage. You are no doubt surprised that I know where you've been. It seems that there's an awful lot I need to explain to both of you which is why I am here. I need you to come with me tomorrow. We will be heading for Childerley Waters in Cambridgeshire where there is an outreach Cold Crimes Ops Resource.'

'Why?'

'I think it's time you both knew a little more about what happened to your respective parents. If you were aware of all the facts then the scene at Stiffkey could have been avoided.'

'You mean with Lev Baranski?'

'Lev Baranski is a young man who has lost his father. You lost your father. There was bound to be some kind of stand-off.'

Rose narrowed her eyes at James Munroe. He was talking as though it was just Brendan who was involved. What about her mother, Kathy Smith? Hadn't James Munroe told her that he had known her mother from when she first joined the police force? Didn't he have anything to say about her?

'It was you people who cleared out the cottage?' Joshua said. 'Who moved the boat?'

'We can't have anything like this happen again. You both need to know the whole truth and that is why you will come with me tomorrow to Childerley Waters. I've already spoken to your grandmother, Rose. I will send a car for you and then it will pick up Joshua.'

'No,' Joshua said. 'We'll come in our car. That all right, Skeggs?'

Skeggsie nodded. James Munroe sighed.

'You have GPS? I can give you coordinates.'

He pulled out a pad from his pocket and wrote out a postcode.

'Look it up on Google Maps. It's an out of the way place but all the better to have a research facility there. Shall we meet there at, say, eleven o'clock? It's about an hour's drive from here, give or take the traffic. Here is my card. My mobile number is on it. I already have yours, Rose.'

'*You* got my text? What about Frank Richards?'

'Ah, Frank. That's another bit of the story. You will find it all out tomorrow. There will be documentation. At last, Rose, Joshua, we are in a position to tell you what we know. Eleven o'clock.'

He stood up. 'I'll see myself out.'

'Until tomorrow. I'll see myself out.'

He walked out of the kitchen. Rose stood still. Joshua followed after him.

'He got here about ten minutes before you,' Skeggsie said. 'Like he knew you were about to arrive. I left him in the hall. I put all our stuff away. He never saw a thing. Not one thing.'

The front door slammed and then there was the sound of Joshua coming back up the stairs.

'What about that? We are definitely getting somewhere. A senior policeman is going to *tell us the truth*.'

'I wouldn't be too sure about that,' Skeggsie said.

But Joshua's face was rapt. Rose saw excitement there. Rose didn't feel the same. She felt a kind of foreboding. Five years before Chief Inspector James Munroe had told her the truth. *Your parents are most certainly dead, killed by an assassin, paid for by organised crime.*

Now even though he no longer worked as a policeman he had something else to tell them. A new truth.

She did not trust him.

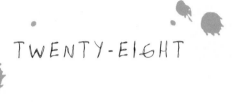

TWENTY-EIGHT

The journey to Childerley Waters took just over an hour. They arrived early and found themselves a couple of miles outside a village, sitting at the perimeter fence of a place called The Cambridge Centre. It was a square one-storey brick building about the size of a tennis court. In front of it was a parking area, the lines of each space sharply painted. The tarmac was smooth, no weeds or ruts. It looked pristine – as if it had never been driven on. The windows of the building had vertical blinds which looked crisp and smart. The entrance doors were closed.

There wasn't any sign of life.

The fence was solid and the only way in was via a gate on top of which was a CCTV camera. At the side of the gate, at about the height of a driver, was a speaker pad. A red light blinked on and off. It was the only sign of activity in the whole place.

They parked across the lane from it and sat and waited. There was tension in the car. The mix of anxiousness and excitement they had felt the previous evening had flattened out on the drive. Skeggsie had driven and the satnav had guided them there. Skeggsie coughed from time to time in between the monotone voice telling them to *Keep ahead, Join the motorway* or *Take the third exit at the roundabout*. Joshua was the only one who had a lot to say. He said he had spent all the previous night thinking about the notebooks so he talked about national security, spies, and international terrorism. The fact that James Munroe was no longer a policeman had given him fuel for his theories. 'He's a civil servant!' he said over and over. 'That's code for the secret service. Spooks.'

Rose had spent most of the previous evening thinking about her mum and Brendan and the sudden appearance of the ex-policeman. From time to time her thoughts had been interrupted by the events surrounding Rachel Bliss's death. She wondered what had happened to Molly. The idea of her being arrested seemed cruel and unjust yet she *had* pushed Rachel into the water. She *was* the cause of Rachel's death. She'd pictured all the girls at lunch as they'd had been on the previous Friday when she'd first arrived. The news about Molly Wallace would be the main topic of conversation. They would all look at Molly in a new way, in awe of what she'd done and scandalised by the results of her actions.

Her grandmother, Anna, had spent some time with her, telling her about ex-Chief Inspector Munroe's phone call and his wish to inform them all about what had happened to Kathy Smith and Brendan Johnson. Rose and Joshua were to be told first. Then Munroe had told Anna that he would visit her in the afternoon and give her the relevant information about her daughter. Anna was slightly miffed that she was not to be included in the trip to Childerley Waters but she said that she had patience and she would wait. At last she would know what had happened to Kathy.

Rose was apprehensive about what James Munroe would say.

That morning, when she was waiting for Skeggsie to come and pick her up, she got cold feet. She didn't want to go. The previous few days had drained her and she didn't know if she wanted any more emotional turmoil. When the car pulled up she said goodbye to Anna and left, pulling her grey coat around her and putting a black wool hat on her head.

Now, sitting in the Mini waiting for James Munroe, Joshua and Skeggsie had gone quiet. They had ten minutes or so until the meeting time. Rose was in the back and she looked out of the window at The Cambridge Centre and wondered what story they were here to find out about. The last thing they had heard from Frank Richards was that her mother and Joshua's father were alive. Rose had a terrible feeling inside her that this would not be confirmed today. She stared at the building, her eyes trying to make some sense of it. There was a stillness about it, as if nothing had ever happened there. The lane was silent; no cars had passed since they'd parked. The trees were static, not a breath of wind anywhere. There was a funereal mood. Even Joshua looked gloomy.

Skeggsie was using a blue inhaler sucking some drug into his lungs as a black car came slowly up the lane.

'Here he is,' Joshua said, sitting up.

The black car passed them and Rose expected it to turn into the entrance to The Cambridge Centre. Instead it pulled in front of them and James Munroe got out of the driver's seat and walked towards their car. He ignored Skeggsie and went round to the passenger window which Joshua had opened.

'You need to follow me. It's a five-minute drive. Then we'll talk.'

James Munroe did not wait for an answer. He walked back to his car and got in. Then he slowly moved off. Skeggsie followed him.

There was anticipation in the car. Rose was craning her neck to see where they were going. She undid her seat belt and moved to the centre of the back seat so that she could see more easily. A padded envelope was in the way and she picked it up. It was the letter she'd received from Rachel Bliss's grandparents. She'd forgotten to take it out of the car the previous evening. She shoved it aside and leant forward between Joshua and Skeggsie, looking straight ahead to see what they were heading for.

In spite of her previous gloomy thoughts there was excitement in her chest. She put a hand on Joshua's shoulder and gripped it. Joshua put his over the top of hers and held it there, his clasp strong and warm. Looking up at the rear-view mirror she caught Skeggsie's eye. He held her look for a few seconds. There was something all knowing about Skeggsie. As if he had read her emotions and knew that her feelings for Joshua had got out of her control. She withdrew her hand aware that the black car had its indicator on and was turning off the lane on to a track.

'Remember what we said last night. Whatever he tells us we don't mention *The Butterfly Project* nor the notebooks. We can talk about Frank Richards and the Russians because he probably already knows about that but the rest we keep to ourselves.'

No one spoke. No one needed to. They'd gone over this the previous evening.

They turned into the lane and passed a public footpath sign and another which said *Childerley Waters*. Underneath were the words *South East Hydration Services. Please keep to the paths.*

'We heading for a reservoir?' Joshua said.

'No,' Skeggsie said. 'These are old chalk pits that have been filled up. They are used for some water systems but mostly its unofficial sports and boating facilities. There're a few companies who use this as a place for trainee scuba-diving. I researched it.'

Rose saw the car in front turn again, going slowly, on to an even narrower lane, the foliage dense, the branches of trees hitting the car.

Old chalk pits that had been filled with water. Rose felt a terrible feeling come over her. She didn't like the idea that this place was somehow associated with her mother and Brendan. She sat back in the seat, no longer keen to see where they were going. A great pool seemed to form at the back of her throat and she swallowed a few times.

The black car stopped.

The Mini pulled over and parked.

They got out, Rose waiting until Skeggsie had pulled his seat forward. Once out of the car the three of them stared off to the right. A vast pool of water sat there, like a lagoon. The edges of it were rocky and grey and there was none of the green foliage that surrounded the boating lake at Mary Linton. It looked bleak, the water still and dark. Far away, across on the other side, she could make out some canoes and a larger motor boat pulling a waterskier.

'What is this?' Joshua said.

James Munroe was standing holding a brown file. Rose looked sideways and could see the word *Classified* on it. She was reminded of Lauren Clarke's words the previous day. *They must have been important people, Rose.* Only now did she register that the police officer had used the past tense. *Have been; in the past; no more.*

'Why don't you get into my car? It's warmer there.'

'Skeggs is coming,' Joshua said, hooking his thumb at Skeggsie.

James Munroe nodded.

Somehow Rose ended up in the front next to the ex-Chief Inspector. She sat sideways so that she could see Joshua and Skeggsie. When she looked back to the front all she saw was a flat plain of water stretching away to the horizon. On the Norfolk mudflats they hadn't seen any water even though they'd been close to the sea. Here, in the middle of the country, there was water as far as the eye could see.

'I know that over the last couple of months you and Joshua and your friend have been researching the disappearance of your parents. Indeed, this is all rather coincidental. Recently certain mysteries about their disappearance have been solved. There was no way I wanted to inform you of this until I was completely sure.'

'Why is it anything to do with you?' Joshua said. 'I thought you weren't in the police any more.'

'Not on the operational side, no. I am a civil servant with responsibilities for certain aspects of policing.'

'National security? Foreign relations? Spies?'

Joshua simply couldn't wait. He had to lay all his cards down on the table. At once.

James Munroe shook his head.

'If you let me talk I will tell you what we've found out.

The real detail of it is in this file. This is for you to examine in your own time. My number at the Home Office is there should you want to contact me. I will be available for you. This is a direct line to me.'

Joshua looked like he wanted to say something more but he didn't. Rose looked past James Munroe to the water beyond. It lay like silk, as if it could be cut through with a pair of scissors.

'Your parents were looking at the cold case of five teenage girls who had been suffocated in the back of a container lorry in 2003. They were part of some people trafficking scams that had been taking place. These girls ranged from thirteen to sixteen. They came from Kyrgyzstan, Uzbekistan, Belarus. Two of them were never even claimed. No parents came forward, no one was connected to them. Those two were eventually buried in a Whitechapel cemetery.'

Rose listened hard. She was tensing herself for the end of this story.

'Your parents linked this case to Viktor Baranski, a so-called Russian businessman who lived in Kensington with his family. Respectable. Former Russian navy, rumoured to have sold secrets to the British government. All nonsense we thought. A front. He was a gangster who trafficked young people and sold them around the UK and Europe for as much as he could get. In 2006 it looked like we had a good case against Baranski. Indeed, a lot of it was resting with the Crown Prosecution Service. We had to be sure we could get him and then – out of the blue – he disappeared and days later was found in the sea at Cromer.'

There wasn't a sound in the car.

'The problem was Baranski owed money to some bigger gangsters. German. Two million pounds. When Baranski's body washed up the Germans thought that Kathy and Brendan had deliberately informed the Russian secret service so that they could get their hands on Baranski's money. The Germans wanted that money back. They wanted Kathy and Brendan.'

Two million pounds. It sounded like Monopoly money. Rose imagined it piled up on the table, next to the board.

'So they had to disappear. Look as if they'd gone out of the country. It had to look as though they'd run off with money. That's why they had to leave both of you behind. No one would think it was a put-up job if they left their children behind. Three or four weeks, that's what we thought it would take to flush out these gangsters. It was a really important case. Your parents' lives were in danger and actually so would yours have been if we hadn't caught up with the people that Baranski owed money to. We liaised with the police in Germany and there were traps set to try and catch the people in the organisation. Meanwhile Brendan and Kathy came back from Warsaw under false names and stayed in the cottage in Stiffkey. They were supported by us. Three weeks went by and the

German operation concluded successfully. We were about to take them out of hiding when . . .'

'What?'

'They vanished.'

Rose made a noise in her throat. A kind of childish exclamation. To hear that they had disappeared for a second time was too much. Too much for one daughter to bear.

'We looked everywhere for them. We searched every single place we could. There was nothing left of the Baranski empire, just the son and his family and the restaurant. The German end had been concluded and we had an empty cottage and two children who had no mother or father. It was a dismal day.'

'So you don't know where they are or what happened to them?' Joshua said, looking down at his knuckles.

'They had access to a car, a silver Audi. It wasn't at the cottage; it was parked in a garage in Holt. When we went to check it was gone. We've kept looking for them. We've never stopped.'

'Frank Richards says they're alive.'

James Munroe shook his head irritably.

'Frank was the support person in Stiffkey. He looked after them for three weeks. He's never seen them since. He's a loose cannon, a maverick. He doesn't know what he's talking about.'

'Why are we here? Why have you brought us to this place?'

'I want to show you something. Come with me. Here, put this in your car, for safe keeping.'

He handed the *Classified* file to Skeggsie. They got out of the car and waited while he put the file in the Mini. Then they all walked down the track towards the water's edge. It took five minutes or so. There were tyre marks down to the water's edge. Joshua was looking at them.

'People bring their sailing boats here. On a *windy* day,' James Munroe said, as if anticipating a question. 'And you can see how close this place is to The Cambridge Centre, the Cold Cases centre. Anything that happens here might be a direct message for the Cold Cases team. *Look, we can do this, even on your doorstep.*'

Something was gripping Rose's arm. She looked down to see that it was her own hand.

They got to the edge of the water and stood looking in. The flat black surface looked solid, like a gel. Rose wondered how deep it was. She was going to ask but suddenly she couldn't speak because she knew she was going to cry.

'Four weeks ago a diver located a car at the bottom of the quarry. It was a silver Audi and it matched the registration number of the car which your parents had access to. There were the remains of two bodies inside the car. Male and female. DNA tests are still taking place to positively identify the people concerned and find out the cause of their deaths.'

Rose turned away. She felt the ground go beneath her feet.

In her heart she'd known they were dead five years ago. But recent weeks had thrown up real doubt and she had begun to hope again. Now it was as if she was that twelve-year-old girl again and James Munroe was in Anna's drawing room sitting across the coffee table from her and telling her to be a brave girl.

She had lost her mother once. It had broken her heart.

Now it was going to happen all over again.

TWENTY-NINE

The flat in Camden seemed cold and bare. For the first time since she'd rekindled her relationship with Joshua she wanted to leave and go home to Anna's house. She couldn't, though. James Munroe was going to see Anna and she didn't want to be there when he visited. She pictured him dressed in black with a top hat; the chief mourner. In her mind he would always be associated with death. Five years before he'd told her to take the news like a grown-up. Now that she was grown-up she took it as though she was a five-year-old child.

Anna would sit in one of her winged chairs in the drawing room and hear a replay of what he'd told them earlier. She'd have her legs neatly crossed and her fingers laced through each other, her manicured nails glossy like jewels.

Maybe Anna would weep. Rose didn't want to be there for that.

In the car, on the return journey from Childerley

Waters, Joshua was stonily silent. Rose cried noisily. She sniffed and blew her nose and cleared her throat. When she dried up she stared out at the passing countryside. Every now and again her body gave an involuntary shiver, an aftershock of so much upset.

'Don't believe him just because he was once a policeman,' Skeggsie had said, coughing from time to time.

But Skeggsie's view of policemen was tainted. His father had been in the force and Skeggsie was sceptical because of all the stories he'd heard.

So Rose cried again. Her skin was wet, her eyes were swollen and she let it go on and on. When they reached Camden her head felt bigger than its normal size, her eyelids raw. She went straight to the bathroom and ran some cold water into the sink. She sat on the corner of the bath and cupped it up with her hands and held it against her eyes. When she'd dried her eyes she found Skeggsie and Joshua sitting at the kitchen table. In the middle of the table was the file marked *Classified*. It looked like one of the files that she used for her college work. Inside it was the flat plain truth that they had wanted for five years. *If only we knew the truth*, they'd said over and over. *We just want to know what happened*, they'd said.

Now they did and it gave little comfort.

Forensics could not give an exact amount of time that the silver Audi had been in the water. The best estimate was four to five years. The investigation was still open-ended but it was James Munroe's view that Kathy and Brendan had been taken from the cottage at Stiffkey and murdered soon after.

The file contained the detailed notes, yet it sat on the table untouched. Joshua who had been the prime mover of the search for their parents didn't reach for it, hadn't opened it, wasn't interested. Skeggsie looked as though he would have liked to open it but held back. It was Rose who had to reach for the file. Rose, who had been reluctant to get involved in the search for their parents, who had dealt with her grief and wanted to let the dead lie in peace. But she'd been seduced by Joshua's fervour. She'd been pulled along in spite of her reluctance only to find that she had to go through the grieving process all over again. She opened the flap of the file and pulled out a wad of papers. On top was a photograph of the car. Her breath skipped in her throat as she saw it. It had been taken at the place where they'd stood hours earlier, Childerley Waters.

The shot had been taken from a distance. The silver car was being pulled out of the water. She thought of Rachel Bliss being lifted out of the lake by the gardener and the groundsman. The photo in her hand showed a big tow truck. There were pulleys attached to the back of the Audi and it was being dragged up from where it had sat in the depths for so long. There were people round, a frogman, a police officer, the man who was working the machinery.

She placed the photograph on the table in plain view but Joshua did not reach for it.

'Will there be a funeral?' she said suddenly.

No one answered.

She wanted to go back to Anna's. She wanted to be anywhere but here.

'I'll go out and get some food,' Skeggsie said, standing up. 'We might as well eat.'

'I'll come with you,' she said.

Joshua got up and walked out of the kitchen. She heard his bedroom door close. She frowned and was about to follow him when Skeggsie touched her arm.

'Leave him to deal with it on his own.'

They shopped, walking round the streets of Camden. They bought bread and salad and a cooked chicken. Skeggsie picked up some fruit and some crisps and a bag of doughnuts.

'Comfort food,' he said.

'Do you really not believe the policeman's story?' Rose said as they were carrying the stuff back.

'I don't know,' Skeggsie said. 'I just know from what my dad said that there's a lot that goes on that the public know nothing about. This James Munroe, why isn't he a policeman any more? How come he didn't come to Joshua and you with this information until you both went to the cottage? There are a lot of unan-swered questions.'

'But they are dead? My mum and Brendan. You do think that now?'

'Maybe. It doesn't answer any of the big questions, though.'

'I'm not interested in any of the big questions. The only thing I'm interested in is whether my mum is alive. And Brendan.'

'What about Frank Richards and the notebooks? You know I found one of the codes. It's a page number, line number, letter number. So if the code is 892 it's page 8, line 9, letter 2. So maybe that letter is 'A'. Trouble is the next time there is an 'A' it will be a different number. Do you see? I've got the computer doing it but every few words it turns into gobbledygook so that means the order has changed. So 892 becomes page 2, line 9, letter 8 which turns out to be a 'P' or something. So far I've deciphered about half a page and it's all about Stiffkey and tides, blah, blah . . .'

They were walking back to the flat and Rose blew through her teeth. Did Skeggsie really believe that she wanted to hear this stuff now? Did he have any sensitiv-ity to what she or Joshua was feeling? The trouble was his involvement with the notebooks had always been academic, never emotional. He looked at the whole thing as a kind of mathematical puzzle. That surprised her in a way because he was an art student. She'd have thought that he might have been *affected* more. Joshua was his closest friend and yet he did seem to experience things in a dispassionate way. Skeggsie's art was a bit like that. There were no paintings or sculptures around. Skeggsie's art was on his computer; animation, films, photography, installations.

They passed the Mini where they'd parked earlier.

'I do care, you know,' Skeggsie said, as if reading her mind.

She shrugged. Skeggsie stopped at the car.

'What's that?' he said, taking the keys out, opening the Mini's door with a pop.

He leant into the back of the car and pulled out the padded envelope that Rose had left there the day before. Rose tutted at the sight of it. She'd forgotten it again. She took it from Skeggsie, folded it in half, and pushed it into one of the carrier bags.

They returned to the flat. The kitchen was still empty. Rose walked up to Joshua's bedroom door and opened it a crack. He was lying on his side on the bed. His eyes were closed.

'Let's get the lunch. He'll wake up soon,' Skeggsie said from down the hall.

They moved round the kitchen quietly. Skeggsie put the chicken on a baking tray and covered it with tin foil and put it into the oven. Rose sorted out the salad and cut some bread. She opened the crisps and put them in a bowl in the middle of the table and laid some plates out. The activity made her feel better. When she heard movement from the other room she cheered up a bit. Once Joshua was up they could eat. Maybe they could start afresh and leave this awful thing behind them. Move on with their lives. Of course, Rose wished her mother was alive but if she truly wasn't then she had to go forward, had to walk away from this heavy sorrow that she'd carried all these years. The blip of hope they had had now looked like some bad joke. Frank Richards had been a siren pulling them on to the rocks.

She picked up the *Classified* file and took it into Skeggsie's room. She placed it on the table where they usually kept the notebooks stuff, although it was now clear, the notebooks and printouts hidden away by Skeggsie after James Munroe arrived.

She went back into the kitchen and picked up the envelope from Rachel Bliss. She didn't want to open it but she knew she would. If she'd taken the other letters seriously then she might have been able to help Rachel. Instead her hatred of the girl had meant she'd ignored her calls. If she was truly going to move on from what had happened these last few months she needed to see what Rachel's message was. She pulled at the opening and the flap came away from the envelope. She put her hand in and pulled out some photographs. There was a note as well and she flicked her eyes over it.

Dear Rose, I took these today to prove to you that I was telling the truth. Rachel.

It was brief, for Rachel, none of the histrionics she had got used to. She looked at the photographs. At first glance they seemed to be of someone holding a newspaper. Three A4 size photographs of the top or corner of a newspaper with people in the background.

What was it?

'This is weird,' she said out loud.

Then she looked at the note again and saw a date at the top of it. 10th June.

'This was written to me on 10th June. Five months ago. What is it? I don't get it.'

Joshua had come into the kitchen. He was stretching his arms up in the air. His hair was sticking out at the side. He looked a little better, *softer* for the sleep he'd had.

'Rachel Bliss wanted to send this to me seven months ago but she never posted it. It's some odd photographs of people at the seaside and there's this newspaper at the bottom of every one as though she hasn't framed the shot properly.'

'Let's have a look,' Skeggsie said.

Skeggsie took the photos. Rose looked at the brief letter again. *I took these today to prove to you that I was telling the truth.* 10th June. Just after the exams, a couple of days before she left Mary Linton for good. Rose thought back to the day when Rachel came and sat beside her in the quad and told her that she'd seen her mother and step-father on the pier at Cromer. It had just been another of Rachel's lies and Rose had given her short shrift.

'It might be that the newspaper's been deliberately put in the photo to give the date. You know like they do in ransom videos. To prove the kidnapped person is still alive on a certain date. Proof of life?' Skeggsie said.

'Ransom videos. You've been watching too many movies lately,' Joshua said grimly.

Rose snatched the photos back from Skeggsie. She put them all flat on the kitchen table. She pushed the plates and the salad and the crisps out of the way.

'Have you got a magnifying glass?' she said.

Skeggsie nodded.

'Can I have it?' she said shrilly.

'A *please* would be nice,' Skeggsie mumbled.

She looked hard at the first photograph. Then the others. Her breath stopped in her throat as she saw them. They were on deckchairs, by the steps that went up from the beach to the promenade. The man was sitting reading a newspaper. He had dark glasses on and a sun hat but still Rose knew him.

'Give me the magnifying glass, quick.'

'What you doing, Rosie?' Joshua said.

She held it over the man's face and let out a gasp of recognition.

The woman's face was clearer. In the first photograph she was pulling her hair back into a tie. In the second she was standing up, brushing sand from her front. In the third she was staring out to sea, her face pensive. Rose didn't need the magnifying glass to know who it was but she used it, anyway. Her mother's face seemed to rise out of the picture towards her. Her mother, sitting with Brendan on Cromer beach five months before.

'Rosie, are you crying? What is it?' Joshua said, sounding concerned.

She stood back and handed the magnifying glass to Joshua. Her tears were mingling with the widest smile she could manage.

'Look,' she said. 'Look for yourself!'

Skeggsie looked puzzled. Joshua took the magnifying glass. After a few moments he seemed to speak directly to the photographs, his fingers running over the images as if he could actually touch the people in them.

'Dad,' he said.

After all the lies Rachel had told she had finally come up with the truth. Rose closed her eyes. 'Thank you,' she said softly.

THIRTY

There was no funeral, just a memorial service.

It was in a small church in Hampstead. Anna arranged it and Rose had to attend. It was to be a small affair – just a few close friends and a chance for Anna to say goodbye formally to her daughter Katherine. Anna tentatively asked Rose if it would be all right if she had a photograph and flowers dedicated to *Katherine Christie* as that was the name that Anna had known her daughter by. Rose did not object. Rose was supportive. Joshua had argued that it was the right thing to do in the present circumstances. James Munroe had helped Anna with the arrangements. He had told her that it should be low-key as investigations were still going on. He had explained the bodies could not be released as they were still part of the investigation.

Anna had seemed buoyed up by the event and had talked to Rose a few times about her daughter. In the past she'd said hurtful things about how Katherine had left home, changed her name, became a career woman and had a baby. How she'd rejected Anna's way of life and did what she wanted to do. Anna had seen this as a betrayal and had seemed more upset about that than the fact that Katherine had gone missing five years before.

She'd even blamed Brendan Johnson, suggesting that he had murdered Katherine and then gone into hiding himself. Rose had never told Joshua this so it was a shock when Anna came down the garden to Rose's studio and knocked on the door when Joshua was there with her, a few days after the visit to Childerley Waters.

She'd shaken Joshua's hand and said, *I'm sorry for your loss.*

She also told Rose to invite him up to the house at any time.

Anna's acceptance of Munroe's story about Kathy and Brendan's death meant that Joshua was no longer the son of a murderer.

But it was all lies. The story about the car and the people in it was untrue. Rose had struggled with it in the days after they'd seen Rachel Bliss's photographs. She had a hard time believing that ex-Chief Inspector James Munroe had actually lied to them.

'Could it have been a mistake?'

'DNA,' Skeggsie answered curtly.

No mistakes had been made, no errors. It was a made-up story. Rose and Joshua knew it because they had seen three photographs of their parents on Cromer beach five months before, four and a half years after they were supposed to have drowned in a car in Childerley Waters. Munroe was a liar.

On the morning of the memorial service Joshua came to the front of Anna's house and Rose let him in, leading him up to her study.

'I just don't think I should have let this go ahead,' Rose said.

Joshua sat in the armchair. He looked around the room admiringly.

'I should have told Anna the truth. She's going through this and it's a charade.'

'Remember what we said. We have to make Munroe think that we believe every word he said. He is the key to this.'

'But Anna is mourning my mother . . .'

'Rosie, we have to keep our heads here. We stumbled on something really important to Munroe, something to do with our parents and Viktor Baranski and the British police. We found the cottage, the boat, we got Lev Baranski involved. Frank Richards was looking after you, he said, and he gave you the phone number and you used it and it shook everything up. The *Classified* file? It's a work of fiction. But at least now we know. This is not to do with the secret Service or national security. This is to do with the police. If you tell your gran then she will make a fuss and Munroe will know. He'll go to ground and we'll never find out another thing about what happened to them.'

They were holding it all by a slender thread. A book of butterflies that held the key to the notebooks they had taken from Frank Richards. Each notebook concerned a murder; a teenage boy called Ricky Harris and a Russian businessman, Viktor Baranski.

'We have to hold our nerve here, Rosie.'

Rose nodded. It was the right thing to do but it felt wrong.

There were a dozen or so of Anna's friends in the tiny church. Rose and Joshua sat a couple of rows back. Up at the front was a photo of her mother that she hadn't seen before. It was when she was a teenager, not much older than Rose. Anna had had it blown up. It was Katherine, the teenage girl Rose had never known. Her hair was full and styled and she had lipstick on and looked a little like Anna herself. Rose wondered if she was wearing clothes from Bond Street. Soon after that photograph Katherine left her mother and became Kathy Smith.

The church door opened and Rose and Joshua looked round. It was James Munroe, wearing his Crombie, carrying a small bunch of flowers. Rose felt Joshua stiffen beside her. Munroe walked up the aisle and nodded to them. Then he went into a pew on the other side.

The service was short with a mix of prayers and readings from the Bible and Shakespeare. At times Rose felt her eyes prickle as though she was on the brink of crying. Then she made herself stare at her mother's photo on the altar rail. Katherine Christie was someone she never knew. In her purse Rose had a square photograph cut from a larger one. Her mother, Kathy Smith, staring out to sea on a beach in Cromer five months before. Alive.

As the service wound up she noticed Munroe edging along the pew and making his way down the other side of the church. Watching him steal away, she felt Joshua's hand grab hold of hers. He squeezed it tightly, leant down to her ear and whispered to her.

'We'll find them.'

She turned to him nodding, the beginnings of a sob coming out of her mouth. She threw her arm around his neck and hugged him tightly. He was right. They would keep looking until they found them.